She watched it glide away, a long white shape cutting
gracefully through the water. Bubbles foamed back
from its strong shoulders, and what she had taken
for weed was hair, she realised now. A mane...
It was a horse! A swimming horse. A water horse,
galloping away down the canal.

Also by Holly Webb

Rose Series

Rose
Rose and the Lost Princess
Rose and the Magician's Mask
Rose and the Silver Ghost

Lily Series

Lily
Lily and the Shining Dragons
Lily and the Prisoner of Magic
Lily and the Traitor's Spell

www.holly-webb.com

Holly Webb

ORCHARD

ORCHARD BOOKS
Carmelite House
50 Victoria Embankment
London EC4Y 0DZ

This edition published in 2015 by Orchard Books

ISBN 978 1 40832 762 3

Text © Holly Webb 2015

A CIP catalogue record for this book is available from the British Library.

1 3 5 7 9 8 6 4 2

Typeset in Adobe Caslon by Avon DataSet Ltd,
Bidford-on-Avon, Warwickshire

Printed and bound by CPI Group (UK) Ltd, Croydon, CR0 4YY

The paper and board used in this book are from wood from responsible sources.

Orchard Books is an imprint of Hachette Children's Group and published by
The Watts Publishing Group Limited, an Hachette UK company.

www.hachette.co.uk

For Tom, Robin
and William

CHAPTER ONE

THE GIRL IN THE KINGFISHER blue dress dipped and swirled and spun across the floor, with the young boy laughing and twirling after her. Her mask was a glittering bird, to match her feathered dress, and his was a fox, sharp-nosed, with silver wire whiskers. He didn't know who she was, but he had asked her to dance after he saw her swipe a fingerful of cream from the top of one of the elaborate trifles on the supper table. She had seen him watching, and she'd looked so guilty, even under the mask, that he'd laughed out loud, and she had laughed too.

'Shall we dance the next one?' he asked her eagerly, and brushed a kiss across her hand.

But then her dark eyes behind the mask clouded, and she muttered an excuse and hurried away, leaving him standing in the middle of the floor.

Had he offended her, asking for another dance? He watched her dart through the crowds and away into another room and sighed. He would go and wait by the supper table, to see if she came back.

But the girl in the kingfisher dress had flung herself through the laughing, dancing partygoers to a discreet little side-room. It was reserved for ladies who found themselves caught short, and needed help with their hundred-layered petticoats, and stiff satin skirts. She shut the door, and leaned on it, wishing she hadn't let that boy swing her round and round so fast. All that cream, on top of crystallised fruits. She should have been more careful. It was just so exciting not to be a princess, for a night. Everyone wore masks on New Year's Eve, it was the tradition, and Venice was a city that lived by its traditions.

If he'd known who she was, he would have treated

her like the blown glass from the islands. He wouldn't even have dared to touch her hand – let alone kiss it.

The young servant girl left in charge of the room didn't recognise Olivia for the princess either, not in her jewelled bird mask, topped with its crown of gleaming feathers. There were several other little birds dancing in the halls, and the girl dipped a sketchy curtsey, and smirked as Olivia snatched at a basin, and sank into a chair, gulping painfully. It was no good. She fought at the ribbon ties and tore off her mask to be quietly sick.

Then she caught the maid's eye as she looked up, and saw the expressions flit across the girl's face. Shock. Fear that she had been rude. And was that excitement, just a little, at being so close to the princess?

But mostly there was a sharp, undisguised look of dislike.

Why did the girl hate her so?

Olivia blinked, and the maid suddenly busied herself tidying away the basin, and fetching a delicate glass of cool water with lemon peel, and a bowl of warm water for the princess to wash her hands.

She didn't look up at Olivia again.

The strangeness of that look hid what had happened for a moment, but as Olivia lay back in the chair and watched the girl scurry about, she realised that she felt quite odd. Not ill – this was a clearness in her head. A sharpness to her thoughts – perhaps it was why she had noticed the girl's angry face. Usually she wouldn't even have cared. She didn't look at servants, why would she?

As she patted her cheeks with a scented cloth, and dabbed perfume in the hollows of her neck, Olivia realised that everything felt different. Things were… brighter. It was the only way she could describe it – as if a layer of dust had been swept away. Pretty, glittery dust, but dust that had still softened and furred the edges of her thoughts.

A dust that had bewitched her since she was tiny. A spell – lots of spells – floating away into the air like glittering dust motes. She had broken free, when she'd never even known that she was bound…

The water closed over her face, jade green, milky and warm, and she breathed bubbles. Her lungs burned, and she gasped

in water, choking and struggling as the sunlight drifted further away...

'My lady?'

Warmth – a strong body, pushing her back up to the surface...

Someone was standing outside the thick, embroidered curtains and whispering. They were only whispering very, very quietly, of course. It would be most improper for anyone to raise their voice to the daughter of the duke.

Olivia surfaced slowly, dragging herself from deep, watery dreams. She stretched out a pale hand, wafting it vaguely at the heavy brocade. At once, the maid drew the curtains aside. She looked relieved, Olivia thought, trying not to smile. Poor Etta had to make sure Olivia got up, without actually being so rude as to wake her. Sometimes, on those days when she felt bored before she'd even got out of bed, and she knew that there would be an endless round of audiences, and lessons, and council sessions, Olivia pretended she was still asleep, just to see what Etta would do. The servant girl's best effort so far was to waft the scent of Olivia's

11

morning chocolate in through the curtains with one of her own fans.

'Chocolate, my lady?' Etta murmured, balancing the heavy tray on one hip, while she deftly looped back the curtains.

'Please tell me there are biscuits…' Olivia said, wriggling up in bed and blinking. Her eyes felt sticky, and her dreams had been distinctly odd. Unpleasant, she thought, although she couldn't quite remember. She felt as though she'd hardly slept at all.

'Here, my lady,' Etta cooed, passing her a delicately painted plate, laden with scented golden wafers.

Olivia dipped one in her chocolate, and sighed. 'Is it raining?'

'No, my lady.' Etta glanced at her sideways, as though trying to gauge the princess's mood. Would she get snapped at, if she dared more than a straight yes or no answer?

The little princess sucked at the biscuit, and dipped it in again, peering thoughtfully at the curtains on the other side of the bed.

Etta hurried round to pull them back and tie them

12

up out of the way. 'It's quite sunny, my lady,' she murmured. 'Warm.' She darted over to the window shutters, and laid a hand on them questioningly.

Olivia nodded. 'I suppose you'd better,' she said gloomily.

As Etta unlatched the shutters and drew them open, a dancing golden light shimmered over the walls, and caught the gilding on the furniture. Etta smiled as the warmth eased her aching shoulders, but the little princess squirmed and moaned, shielding her eyes from the light. 'So bright, ugh. Still, I suppose we won't be soaked, like last year. It was dismal.'

'My lady, speaking of the ceremony, we should start to get you dressed. If you please,' Etta added hurriedly. 'That gown…'

'Yes, I know, it'll take hours.' Olivia twisted her shoulders, feeling the weight of the dress already. 'At least I only have to wear the stupid thing once a year.'

She sipped her chocolate, watching as Etta bustled around, filling a golden basin with perfumed water, and sprinkling the steaming bowlful with pink rose petals. One poor gardener's boy with a touch of magical talent had to lavish all his attention on those rose bushes, so that there were petals for the princess's washing water all year round, whatever the weather.

It was stupid, really, Olivia thought, as she dipped her fingers into the warm water, and splashed it over her face. Quite useless. The rose petals didn't really *do* anything.

But at the same time, if Etta offered her a bowl without the petals, she would be furious. Certain things were just bred into princesses. Certain expectations.

Etta was opening the door of her wardrobe room now – the size of some of Olivia's dresses meant that a whole room for them was quite necessary. She staggered out with the jewel-encrusted overskirt that Olivia would have to wear today. It was the same one that she had worn for the ceremony the year before, but it would still fit, with a new set of petticoats to make it look a little different. She had not grown much. Or at all. Etta, who was the same age, was at least a head taller.

Olivia climbed down the two steps from her huge, curtained bed, carrying her cup of chocolate, and went to look at the dress. She didn't like it. It made her think of the long, chilly, rather boring ceremony, which she had attended every year since she'd been born. A whole day of ritual and dreary hymn-singing, and smiling, smiling, all the time. This year the Wedding of the Sea would be worse, of course. Olivia dug her nails into her palms, as she found herself thinking wistfully of all the years before, when she had floated through the ceremony half in a dream. It would be so much easier to listen to the spells. To give in. Then she wouldn't feel the heavy brocade of the dress. She'd hardly notice how breathless the corset left her, or the dull aching of her scalp under her ornately dressed hair. It would be *easy* to smile.

I could go and visit my aunt's rooms, Olivia thought to herself, frowning as she picked at the jewels on the skirt, and sipped chocolate. *It would be simple, I could just say I had a headache, or my throat was sore, and did she have anything that would help. I'd just have to look at her, and let her look at me, and I'd forget again. It would be like it used to be. All the sharp edges smoothed away. Everything gentle and sweet…*

But even though the dress would hurt her by the end

of the day, Olivia knew she wouldn't go to her aunt's. She set down her chocolate hard, so the thin china bowl rang against the marble-topped table. It still made her angry, thinking of all those years that she hadn't known what her aunt was doing. And if she hadn't felt so ill on New Year's Eve, she might never have found out.

Someone had given her a box of crystallised fruits, and Olivia had eaten them, all of them, while she was supposed to be lying down and resting, so as to be fresh for the masked ball that night. She had been reading, and she hadn't quite realised that she was eating her way through the box – suddenly there just weren't any left. As the slow, stately dances gave way to a twirling, stamping mass, she had turned greenish-pale behind her mask, and she'd had to slip away to one of the antechambers. And after that, everything had changed.

Olivia had puzzled over it, ever since. How had she broken the spell? Especially since her aunt was so strong – Lady Sofia was the sister of Olivia's father, part of the royal bloodline. Her magic shone in every move she made, every word she spoke. Although only the duke and Olivia, his heir, carried the water magic that was so vital for the city, all the family were strong magicians. Venice was full of people with a touch of magic, like the boy who grew the roses, but the duke's family was far stronger, these days. Their magic had grown as the city grew around them. The great magic of the duke had protected the city, and his people; and the people of Venice had let their own strong magic fade away to pretty tricks and knacks. Now they relied on their rulers for protection instead.

Olivia's father drew his power from the city – the walls were steeped in his magic, and it moved and strengthened with every tide that flowed in from the lagoon. But then the tides flowed out again.

Olivia's hand shook a little as she ran her fingertips over an embroidered bird on the ornate skirt, and its sapphire eyes glinted at her. She would not think about the tides draining out, and sucking the magic away with them.

She wrenched her thoughts back to Lady Sofia. She would not let her aunt slip any more spells around her. She would have to be strong today, be on her guard through the long hours of the ceremony.

Lady Sofia's great strength was a sort of charm, Olivia had decided, over the last few months. She could make people do what she wanted, so easily, and without them realising that they'd ever considered doing anything different. It was immensely powerful.

Olivia had decided eventually that it was pure luck that she had slipped out of her aunt's spell. If she hadn't over-indulged on crystallised cherries, and had to tear away her mask to be sick… If it hadn't been New Year's Eve and nearly midnight, when the magic of the masks was stronger than any charm… If she hadn't let that dark-haired boy from Lord Paolo's household swing her round and round…

She had torn off the mask in a hurry, and her aunt's years of sticky-sweet charms had torn away too. Olivia had been her own self again – not spelled to be quiet and well-behaved and obedient, as she had been ever since she'd emerged from the nursery.

There was a certain way that Lady Sofia used to look at her. Very clear-eyed, so that Olivia felt she would look through her aunt's amber irises, and see beyond to something else. Something so fascinating that she would never look away, just in case she missed it.

I don't look at her now, Olivia thought, twitching the fabric, so that the flower of yellow diamonds under her fingers glittered and glowed in the sunlight. *I know enough to smile, and look the other way, and pretend that that everything's the same. That I don't know what she did. How many times has she done it? I wonder...*

Would a spell like that have worked upon a baby? A tiny child, just walking? It seemed wrong to bewitch a child so small. But then Olivia sighed. Lady Sofia could hardly have let her scream her way through the service, could she?

Not for the first time, Olivia wondered what it was like to be a normal child. Not a princess. Not the heir. It would be...

No. She couldn't actually imagine what it would be like to be Etta, who was still quietly piling up petticoats, ready for Olivia to put on. Or one of the ragged children she might see for only a moment today, before someone whisked them away. Princesses were only allowed to see the beautiful people, and beautiful things – if the royal gondola floated past a scruffy house with peeling paint, someone would probably slide a flower-decked skiff in front of it, before Olivia could be upset.

'My lady?' Etta murmured patiently, holding out the first of the layers of petticoats, and Olivia turned to her, wondering if she could ask her maid what it was like not to be special.

She turned too swiftly, reaching out for the stiff, lace-edged petticoat, and caught the little inlaid table with the sleeve of her chemise – the table she had put her half-empty cup of chocolate on, so she could play with the jewels on the precious overskirt, stretched reverently over a chair just next to her and Etta.

The dark, grainy chocolate slopped out towards the jewelled fabric, and Etta caught her breath in a gasp – she was too well-trained a servant to scream, but Olivia could see that she wanted to. If the dress were ruined, it would be Etta who suffered, not her careless mistress.

'I'm sorry!' Olivia gasped – it was probably the first time she had ever said the words to Etta – and then she closed her eyes, and flicked her fingers at the chocolate.

Etta watched, her cheeks pale.

Of course, Etta knew that the princess was a skilled magician. She saw the princess have lessons in magic every day, along with deportment, and Talish, and needlework, and Venetian history and diplomacy. But Olivia didn't tend to use magic very much at all, and her maid had grown used to thinking of her only as a spoiled, pettish little thing, who hated getting up in the mornings, and had to be helped to dress.

Now the spoiled little girl had silvery fire shimmering around her fingertips, and she had stopped that great disastrous spill of chocolate in mid-air. It was floating – gurgling and swirling about, like smoke, or, or dust. Etta gaped at it, and Olivia opened her eyes, and smiled at her maid.

Etta was the only companion she had, Olivia realised suddenly. She didn't want to lose her because of her own carelessness.

She cupped her glowing hands under the chocolate, and patted at it, as any normal child would pat dough to help shape a loaf of bread. She dabbed at it with delicate, feathery little strokes of her glittering fingers, laughing to herself. And then she handed the end result to Etta.

It looked up at her and mewed.

'A kitten, my lady!' Etta's cheeks flushed pink with delight, as the little creature rubbed its face against her reddened hands. 'Is it…is it *real?*'

Olivia frowned at the kitten thoughtfully. 'What an odd question… He's made of magic, of course. But he'll eat and drink and mew to be let out. I don't know if he will ever grow any bigger, though. He's for you. But if the Lady of the Chambers says anything, you'd better tell her that he's mine, and you're just looking after him because I'm too lazy.' She lifted one eyebrow at Etta, and Etta went even pinker. Olivia looked down at the kitten, and tickled him behind the ears. Etta probably thought that she could read minds, or that she had little fairy spies planted all through the palace to hear her moan. Olivia didn't, though of course she could have listened to the maid's thoughts if she wanted to. But Etta *must* think that she was lazy, sleeping late in a gilded bed, while her maid ran about lighting her fires, and fetching her breakfast. And whatever else it was that servants did. Olivia didn't actually know.

They were just there, they always had been.

Olivia rubbed the tiny creature under his chin. 'Perhaps you had better call him Coco.'

It was lucky she had eaten the biscuits, Olivia thought, wincing as Etta laced up her bodice. The jewelled overskirt was almost too stiff to sit down in – she had to sit carefully, in stages – and she could hardly breathe, let alone eat. Actually, now it was laced so tight, she was almost sure she could see the biscuits, stuck in a lump in her middle, and making the embroidered stomacher bulge. Olivia didn't care. She should have had a couple more, to cheer herself up – even though she was already feeling sick, just a little. And anyway, they'd fed the leftover biscuits to the kitten.

Until now, the ceremony of the Wedding of the Sea had just been a yearly bore, something to be dreaded for uncomfortable clothes, and repeated lectures from Aunt Sofia and the other ladies of the court, on proper behaviour for a princess.

This year, Olivia was frightened.

It had been creeping up on her for a while, ever since

New Year, when she'd lost the gentle cushion of her aunt's spells, but it had taken her ages to work out what the feeling was. It was unfamiliar to her. What would she be frightened of? Olivia understood being angry – she was, often – but fear was new.

There had been a coldness growing deep inside her for weeks now, a stony frightened cold that seemed to spread through Olivia a little more each time she saw her father. It squeezed her insides, and made her gasp. He was paler, slower, more insubstantial whenever they met – which was less and less often now, as though Duke Angelo knew that she could see he was wearing away. Olivia was not sure if her poor, faded father could bear the weight of the city's hopes and fears for much longer. But it was his magic that bound all the many little magics of the city together, and held it all in place. And when he died, it would be passed on to Olivia, that deep power that was the city. It was something that Olivia had always known – it had never worried her before. It was just the way life was – like rose petals in her washing water.

Today the duke would be leading the Wedding of

24

the Sea, the most important ritual there was. And this in a city that was truly built on ceremony and tightly woven magic, like a thin gilding over water and marshland. If the wedding went wrong, the city's fortunes would be blighted for a year, if not for longer. Without the favour of the sea, the city would be lost. Especially now, with the great bulk of huge, power-hungry Talis lurking so very close. The Talish empire was growing every year, swallowing up smaller countries on the borders. They had been wanting to annex Venice for centuries, but the duke's tiny island state had the magic to protect her – that and a fleet of huge warships.

But it was all bound up with the sea. Without the favour of the sea, the magic would lose its salt, and the ships would founder. The Talish would leap at the chance to make Venice part of their great empire, and take her rich trading port and mighty ships for their own.

Olivia frowned as she paced slowly, grandly down the tapestried passageway towards the Grand Chamber. She couldn't have paced fast if she wanted to, the dress was too heavy, and she still couldn't breathe all that well, even though she and Etta had compromised on letting the bodice lacing out a good three-fingers'-width. Etta had been distracted by her pretty Coco, or she wouldn't have given in – she knew her duty, and Lady Sofia was more frightening than the little princess. Olivia hoped she wouldn't be punished for sending her mistress out not looking her best.

The Talish ambassador would be there at the ceremony today. He would be most favourably placed on the royal barge, close to the duke, where everyone could keep an eye on him, nasty old snake that he was. The Talish probably thought that if they invaded Venice, the sea-magic that made Venice so strong would be theirs too, but it wouldn't. Would it? Surely the city's magic was too much its own – and the duke's. Without her father – or her – the Talish would have nothing. Venice would crumble back into mud and marshland within a generation. Or so Olivia had always been taught.

What is wrong with my father? Olivia thought angrily,

as she padded, snail-like, into the Grand Chamber, and ignored the trumpeter who was blowing a fanfare for her.

The chattering hiss of the crowd died away as the court bowed or swept great curtseys as she passed. The room was full, so tightly packed that the ladies' huge dresses pressed against each other as they curtseyed. Every highborn family in the city was there, together with ambassadors from all the courts in Europe. Olivia smiled graciously at the Talish ambassador as he bowed and flashed his yellow teeth back at her. He was placed close to the throne, as she had expected.

Olivia paused to curtsey deeply to her father. The duke sat rigid on his throne, his hands tightly clenched over the lion-heads carved on its arms, so tightly clenched that the bones stood out as pale lumps through his thinning skin.

If only it was easier to talk to him on her own. But it never had been. He had come to her nurseries occasionally when she was little, to see how she was, and he would try awkwardly to play. But he wasn't very good at it, and after a few minutes he would slip away, leaving his young page boys to entertain her instead. Olivia had always wondered if things would have been different if her mother had lived. The duchess had died a year after Olivia was born, and she had no memory of her at all.

But even though they hardly spoke, Olivia had always felt close to her father, through the magic they shared. She could *feel* him loving her, and that had always been enough. The love hadn't weakened, but the magic had. She had been pouring her own magic in to fill the gap between them for months, Olivia admitted to herself, as she looked at her father properly, and tried to gulp back her gasp of dismay.

He smiled faintly, and waved her to the smaller throne that had been placed next to his. Olivia was his heir, and one day, she would rule the city – or her husband would, anyway.

Olivia returned his smile with a gracious princess curving of the lips, and lowered herself carefully on to the chair. Bending was not easy, and Etta had to twitch and pull at the skirts so that Olivia's feet didn't stick straight out in front of her. Then she ducked back

28

behind the throne to wait until Olivia had to get up.

'You look beautiful, my dear,' the duke told her, with a little quirk at the corner of his mouth that made Olivia think he shared her opinion of the dress. He turned his head regally to consult with one of the lords of his council, who was standing on the steps. Olivia stared straight ahead, smiling and smiling, and trying not to bite her lips with worry.

'Your dress is exquisite,' a voice murmured beside her.

Olivia smiled thinly at her aunt, who was posed formally on the steps of the dais with her son and daughter, Olivia's cousins. Lady Sofia was quite good at compliments – she managed to be wonderfully polite, and somehow slightly insulting at the same time. No one could possibly object to being told that their dress was lovely – but Lady Sofia hadn't said anything nice about the girl who was in it.

Lady Sofia was the closest thing to a mother that Olivia had, and she wasn't very close at all. She had directed Olivia's dressmakers and her governesses and her dancing masters for years. Olivia's father saw to

29

her magical education, but everything else was down to her aunt. But all Lady Sofia's affection was lavished on her own two children, Zuan, who was a little older than Olivia, and Mia, a golden-haired toddler, who was standing unnaturally still, her fingers wound in Aunt Sofia's brocade skirt. Mia's eyes were fixed on one of the swirls of woven gold in the fabric, Olivia could tell. If she crouched down next to her little cousin, and looked carefully, she would be able to see the spell that was holding her. It made her shudder, thinking of all the times Lady Sofia had sweetened her the same way, turning her into a biddable little puppet.

Olivia carefully did not look into her aunt's eyes, or Zuan's. She didn't expect Zuan to attempt to enchant her – he was too stupid to try – she just didn't want to be forced to talk to him. They had never liked each other, and as far as Olivia could see, her cousin was only getting worse as he got older. Lady Sofia thought he was perfect, of course.

'Olivia, dear one, is that a little smudge of dust, by your nose?' Lady Sofia purred. 'Look this way for me…' Her voice was lovingly gentle now, and Olivia longed to do as she was told. Her aunt hadn't said anything, in the months since New Year. She had never even given Olivia a sharp look, let alone asked her what she had done to break the spells. She couldn't, Olivia supposed. If Lady Sofia tried to find out what had happened, it would be obvious that she had been trying to control the heir to the throne – trying and *succeeding*. But she hadn't given up. Olivia guessed that her aunt knew the spell had been broken by accident, and she was hoping that Olivia didn't know what she had done, that it was just coincidence that her niece wouldn't look her in the eyes any more.

'Olivia…' Her aunt sounded so kind, and sweet, the way a mother would sound. When she spoke like that, Olivia had always done as she was asked.

Except that she was almost sure that Lady Sofia's honey-voice would smooth away the fear inside her. Olivia had the strangest feeling that the fear was *important*. She did not want it gone.

'Is the court assembled?' Duke Angelo murmured to the counsellor, and the man bowed and nodded. He would have done the same even if the room had been

31

half-empty, as soon as he saw that the duke wished to be gone. The duke's power was so absolute – on the surface at least – that no one would dare to stand up against him.

Olivia smiled again at her aunt, without looking at her, and brushed away the dust that wasn't there. 'I'm sure it's gone, Aunt,' she murmured.

The trumpeter struck up again, and the whispery chatter died away to watchful silence. Olivia was not the only one who had noticed the duke's recent weakness, and his few public appearances. Now his court wanted to see him standing.

Duke Angelo stood, a glorious figure in his purple coat, and long, dark-gold mantle. He offered his arm to Olivia – Etta had given her a discreet push to help her out of the chair – and the pair of them paraded slowly down the steps. In front of them, the royal court divided, drawing back to bow low before their duke, and leave a pathway across the elegant mosaic tiles.

Olivia and her father paced towards the doors that opened out on to the quayside, where the royal barge was moored, ready to take them out into the lagoon.

Olivia's heart beat faster, and she felt a flutter of excitement in her stomach as they came out on to the marble steps, and she saw the great sheet of black water before her. She left the palace so rarely – only every month or so, for a ritual. There were the services in the great church, but that was just a walk through the palace to their own private entrance. She didn't get to go outside. Even though she walked out in the enclosed courtyard for an hour a day, it wasn't the same as being out in the city, or on the water. There were walls, all around, and eyes. It wasn't really like being outside, and on the lagoon, even if she was only going to stand still and wave like a princess.

Her father patted her arm with his thin fingers, and beamed down at her, as though he shared her love of the water. Together, they walked through the crowd of admirers, nodding and smiling as fathers held up their children, and young girls threw flowers under their feet. Here and there a fist was shaken, and Olivia drew back from one grimacing woman, who shouted something angry, about not being able to pay. But the old woman was whisked away by the guards.

'What did she mean?' Olivia whispered, still smiling sweetly, as she had been taught. She didn't remember ever seeing anyone shout at them like that before. But then – what else might she have forgotten? What else had she been spelled into not seeing?

'Nothing…' Her father's own smile stretched a little, and the lines on his face deepened. 'Nothing, my darling. Look, we're there…'

The golden magnificence of the barge should have driven every other thought from Olivia's mind, but she was used to eating from golden plates, and wearing a fortune of lace on her petticoats. Precious metals did not impress her. Besides, it was only gold leaf laid over wood – a ship made of solid gold would sink. So although she beamed and curtseyed to the crowd as they reached the gangplank, she was still remembering the old woman's twisted face.

It reminded her of the girl in the antechamber, the night the spell had been broken. And certain faces she had seen around the palace since, in those moments she stole to wander away from her ladies. Angry faces. Frightened. Distrustful. And always serene and adoring the second she turned back to look, so that she was never quite sure if she'd imagined them.

She walked over the gangplank distractedly, forgetting to be scared as she usually was when the wood creaked and flexed under her feet, and followed her father to the throne under the canopy in the stern of the barge. There she sat, just a little behind him, and looked out at the hundreds of little boats pushing and shoving and darting around the great barge, like puppies trying to play with a huge old dog. The rest of the royal court were coming aboard the barge now, their best clothes sparkling in the sunlight, twittering and whispering like suspicious birds.

Olivia watched them sidelong, seeing the anxious glances directed at her father – anxious but calculating – and then every time a second glance, at her. She had never felt the weight of being a future duchess so heavily before. She didn't *want* to be the heir. All it meant was that before she got to do anything interesting, her father had to die.

CHAPTER TWO

THE BARGE CUT THROUGH the dark water, leaping forward with each deep stroke of the hundred oars. There were oarsmen to man them, of course, but the oars themselves, the whole craft, were full of the magic of the Venetian shipbuilders. The ship seemed to know its own way, out to the deep waters, where a hundred golden wedding rings gleamed, so many fathoms below.

It was a strange old custom, going back as far as the first founders, Olivia's distant ancestors, who had first decided to make their homes in the middle of a marsh, a place so wet that each tussock of grass had to be tied to the next with magic, before one could even think about building a house. Visitors to Venice went home and told their families about the Wedding of the Sea and laughed. But all those who lived in the city knew that they owed their lives to the sea. The wedding was no laughing matter. The gold ring was a present, and at the same time, the line of them snaking across the sea bed was a chain. The sea was chained to the city, as if Venice owned her.

But we only skim about on the surface, Olivia thought, shivering. *There's all that dark water underneath, all through the city. We don't own her at all.* She didn't usually think like this. She loved the water. It always looked so soft and cool and coaxing. Of course, she had never swum in it. She had never so much as dipped her toe in. But the breeze blowing out on the lagoon was always so salty and fresh, and the canals slid by her window like dark silk. So why did the water seem so eerie now?

'Lady Sofia and her quiet little spells,' Olivia whispered to herself. 'She could poison anything.'

There was a gasp, and someone shuffled their feet on

the deck behind her. Olivia looked at her maid sideways, and Etta shifted nervously. The girl had one hand out, as if she wanted – as if she would actually dare! – to put it over Olivia's mouth.

Etta's cheeks were burning, and her eyes looked frightened, Olivia thought curiously. What did her maid know, then, about Lady Sofia and her spells? Olivia hadn't thought Etta understood... But then, Etta saw everything. Her maid was with her almost always, silently watching. She hardly ever spoke to Olivia, and Olivia was almost sure that Etta didn't gossip to the other servants, either. She was just *there* – and Olivia hadn't really noticed her.

'She can't hear us, you know,' Olivia breathed.

Etta spoke to the polished decking, her eyes demurely downcast. 'Are you sure about that?'

'She's all the way over there!'

'Pardon me, my lady, but that means nothing.'

Olivia was silent for a moment, watching her aunt, laughing and gossiping with the other ladies of the court. Even when her aunt was clearly telling a most scandalous story, her eyes were never still. Her head wove from side to side a little too, like a snake's. Olivia shuddered, and lifted one hand, very slightly, feeling the air.

'What are you doing?' Etta hissed.

'I'm seeing if she *is* listening. I don't like being listened to all the time, and pushed here and there with little bits of magic, and told to stay in my rooms and be good. Not just told to. Made to.' Olivia flicked her fingers, stretching out the nails that Etta had polished so nicely with sweet almond oil. She could feel the listening spell, now that Etta had warned her. She could even see it. It glittered, very faintly, like wisps of sea spray, floating in the air. Olivia hissed, very softly through her teeth. How dare someone spy on her! 'There.' She flicked again, and again, feeling the sticky catch of the spell-threads on her fingers as she batted them away. 'Someone was. I don't know if it was her. But now they aren't. So tell me what you know, Etta. Tell me now.'

The pinkness had faded out of Etta's cheeks completely, and her face was wax-candle pale. She glanced up at Lady Sofia again, and then whispered, so

39

quietly that Olivia had to lean back to hear, 'Was that wise, my lady? Won't she know what you just did?'

'Maybe. I don't care. Oh, don't be so feeble, Etta! She'll just think the spell blew away in the wind. It *is* windy out here. Now tell. Has she always done that to me? You were here last year, weren't you?' She frowned, trying to remember when Etta had replaced her previous maid. 'Yes, of course you were. Did she enchant me to behave, when we had this ceremony last year?'

'I think so, my lady,' Etta admitted.

'How can you tell?' Olivia demanded.

'You stopped complaining,' Etta told her simply, and Olivia gaped at her. She wasn't used to being criticised, not straightforwardly like that. If she behaved in a way that her aunt or one of the court ladies disapproved of, they didn't really tell her off. They smiled and smiled, and wrapped any hint of disapproval in so many layers of sugar that sometimes Olivia found it impossible to work out what it was she had actually done wrong.

'And your eyes went funny,' Etta added. 'Like hers.' She jerked her head sideways at Mia, who was so deep

40

in whatever Aunt Sofia had done to her that she was practically falling over.

'If you ever see her doing it again, Etta, promise me that you will pinch me.'

'My lady!'

'If you don't, when I wake up from whatever it is she's done, I will have you...' Olivia trailed off. She knew that there were torture chambers in the very lowest cellars of the palace, and in the prison that was on the other side of the canal, but she wasn't sure exactly what went on in them. It was not a subject for polite conversation. 'Well. You won't like it, anyway,' she added lamely. 'I could probably turn you into something disgusting, if I tried hard enough.'

She glared at the maid. Etta was smirking!

'Don't laugh at me!'

The smirk disappeared at once. 'I know you could, my lady,' Etta whispered back. She patted the side of her skirt, which squirmed a little, and let out the faintest little mew.

'Yes indeed!' Olivia turned back, her own cheeks triumphantly flushed. A little of the frightened hole

41

inside her seemed to have closed up. It had been filled with anger – hate, nearly. The listening spell – so obvious, so easy – had reminded her of the layers and layers of enchantment that Lady Sofia had bound her in for years. How dared her aunt bewitch her? And how much of what Olivia thought she remembered was real?

There was a rush of whispers all around her, and Olivia twitched in her seat. The rolling motion of the oars had stopped, leaving the ship oddly still in the water, poised and waiting. The hush spread outwards over the shoal of little boats, scattered across the lagoon. The same expectant feeling ran through the court as Olivia's father stood, and made a gesture with his bent fingers. The court shuffled slowly to its knees, and Olivia knelt too, the stiffness of her dress forgotten.

The ring appeared before him, tiny and glowing. As it spun slowly in the air, its gold outshone the ship itself, and the heavily embroidered court dresses and twinkling jewels looked cheap and garish.

The choir of children standing behind the duke's golden throne began to sing, their thin, high voices twining with the magic of the ring. It spun faster and faster, and the eyes of all the court were fixed on it.

It was a spell that Olivia had seen her father make so many times before. She knew the words – even the gestures, as he pulled the strength out of the music, and wound it into the glowing light of the ring. The blaze grew stronger, and bigger, like a little second sun floating in the air above the ship, and Olivia wondered how she could have called the ceremony boring, even if she had been half-enchanted every other time. She was caught up in the moment, just like everyone else. A golden happiness shimmered through her, an intense love for the city, and her people, and the sea. She even looked at her cousin Zuan without her usual stab of dislike. He didn't really mean to be nasty. Maybe.

Olivia knelt there on the deck of the barge, smiling at the spell. Her own power was dancing inside her, she could feel her magic longing to join in, to sing with her father's. Maybe he would even let her. She could ask, for next year. Although she was almost sure the spell had to be done by the duke, everyone said so, anyway. It was some terrible omen if not. It would be her one

43

day, though… Olivia blinked that thought away, and let the spell enfold her in its happiness again.

Perhaps Lady Sofia had never had to bespell her to keep quiet for the ceremony after all. She had just imagined it when she was tired and bad-tempered. Surely even little Mia wouldn't cry, with the music swirling round her, and the golden light shining on her face?

Olivia glanced very slightly sideways, to see Mia, and smile at her. She loved her tiny cousin, who would follow her around the palace, hoping for sugared almonds, or a pretty spell to play with.

But the golden lightness inside her sank again as she tried to catch Mia's eye. Her little cousin wasn't even looking at the ring. Her eyes were still fixed on Aunt Sofia's dress, and that strange embroidered pattern. Olivia wanted to leap up, and pull her away. The joy of the spell broke for her a little, and she was suddenly aware of how uncomfortable she was, kneeling on the wooden deck, in her too-tight dress. How funny that Aunt Sofia's small spell to keep Mia quiet and obedient should make Olivia want to yell, and scream, and kick

her aunt overboard. *Later*, she told herself. *Not now.*
Instead she fixed her pretty smile, and turned back to
watch the ring. Soon her father would send it soaring
out over the water, taking all their love with it.

Olivia wanted to stroke it. It looked soft, its gold so
fine and smooth and buttery. But as she watched, the
light dulled, and the ring jolted in the air. It was only
for a second, but Olivia's heart jolted too, and then as
the ring fell out of the air and hit the deck with a ringing,
endless chime, she gasped. The breaking of the spell
was so wrong that it actually hurt. She could feel it deep
inside her, a tearing in her heart. She turned to look at
her father, wondering if he could feel it too.

The duke was standing, staring at the ring, and at his
fingers, as though he didn't understand.

A horrified whisper ran through the court as everyone
leaned forward to see the ring, now spinning slowly,
jerkily on the deck. It was dipping sideways, and
swaying, as though any second it would fall and settle
on the boards.

Her father's face was ashen, and his eyes looked solid
black, with no light in them at all. Olivia couldn't stand

to see him like that. She wanted to leap up and help, but would that be wrong? What if she spoiled the ritual? She glanced around. Would anyone else step forward? His chamberlain? The other powerful magicians of the court? Aunt Sofia?

Her aunt was gazing at the ring in fascinated horror. Olivia reached out to touch her hand. 'Should I...'

Lady Sofia looked over at her brother, and her face twisted – in fear, or anger, Olivia wasn't quite sure. She nodded. 'Yes...'

Olivia swallowed, still unsure. She knew the words, but that was all. That deep magic wasn't inside her – she couldn't do it. She would spoil it! But the spell was dwindling away to nothing now, she could feel it. The soft glow of the metal was fading, and the music sounded thin and sharp. She couldn't let it go on. Stepping forward, she caught her father's hand, and whispered, 'Help...' She wasn't sure who she was calling on. Herself?

Etta shuffled closer to her, and her eyes looked frightened. 'Don't let it break, my lady!'

Olivia squeezed her father's thin hand tighter. Etta

was right. She couldn't leave him standing there alone and lost like this. She stared regally at the astonished faces surrounding them, and smiled.

Her father twitched faintly as she touched him, and he looked down at her, his dull eyes suddenly frantic. 'No...' he whispered. 'No, Olivia, it's too strong, I can't let you...' But he didn't let go of her hand.

Olivia felt the spell seize hold of her, and shake her, like one of her father's hounds, like a delighted dog with a toy. She stood stone-still and smiling, but inside it was flinging her every which way, rolling her over and standing on her in its eagerness.

Then her magic surged up inside her to meet the spell, and the ring began to spin again, and her father's hand grew warmer. His fingers tightened around her own, and she felt the dying magic flicker inside him again.

'It wore you out,' she whispered. 'You should have said...'

She raised her hand, and the ring danced up into the air. As it spun, Olivia felt it reeling out her magic, and she saw that the golden light was her own self, pouring

47

out of her. She laughed delightedly, and the laugh was part of the magic too, her happiness stealing inside everyone who heard it; all the bored, uncomfortably dressed courtiers, the weary oarsmen on the lower deck, and all the townspeople in their tiny boats, spread out across the water.

It was wonderful, and yet it was frightening too, feeling the very essence of herself streaming away into her people. For a second Olivia clenched her fingers, as though to pull it back. What if they took all of her? She would be left empty, dried out like a husk.

That was what had happened, she realised sadly, looking at her father's worn face, skin-over-bone. Almost all of him was gone. It shouldn't be like that, surely? Her father's father, and his father before him – they had gone on performing this ritual for years, and years.

Olivia refused to believe that her father wasn't as strong as his ancestors had been. He was a great magician, she knew it, a great man. Something else was going on. At least now he would have to tell her, surely.

She glared at him determinedly as the ring rose up

higher in the air between them. *You will talk to me!* she thought, as hard as she could. She could make her own father understand when he was standing right next to her, she *could*.

'I will…' he whispered. There was a little clearness in his eyes by now, that thick darkness was lifting. But he still looked exhausted, and she felt his magic waver again as together they hurled the golden ring out over the waters.

All round them there was a whispering, as the duke settled back on to his golden throne, and the singing of the choir rose up again, and the oars began to beat. The ring was falling silently through the water, and the spell had tied the city and the sea together for another year. But it had not been the duke who flung the ring into the sea, but his daughter, and everyone had seen.

'My lady?'

Olivia could hear Etta calling, but it was so much effort to drag her eyes away from the painted tiles. Was she back at the palace, then, already? She didn't remember the journey home from the lagoon at all... She was so tired...

'My lady, wake up!' The fierce tone was something she had never heard from her patient, sweet-natured maid, and it was so surprising that Olivia managed to lift her head and stare.

'They're all looking!' Etta swept a hurried curtsey. 'I'm sorry, my lady.' She raised her voice a little, and started to whine. 'I'm so sorry, my lady, I can't think how that loose thread wasn't noticed, I'll mend it at once, I promise I will...'

'See that you do,' Olivia snapped. 'Careless girl. Be grateful you aren't dismissed.' She waved Etta behind her, and stalked away down the passage from the water door, with Etta scurrying behind, doing her best to sniffle and look guilty.

Once they were safely back in her rooms, Olivia abandoned the ladies-in-waiting in the outer parlour, and growled at Etta to follow her into her bedroom, slamming the heavy door in the faces of her twittering ladies.

'What happened?' she whispered, staring at Etta.

'Last thing I knew, we were out on the water – finishing the ring spell. I don't remember anything else! Tell me what happened!'

Etta gaped back at her, and swallowed uncomfortably. She said nothing.

'I won't be angry, I promise faithfully, Etta. Tell me. Please.' Olivia added the last word almost as an afterthought. It wasn't something she was used to saying. 'Please, Etta… I was…asleep standing up?'

'It seemed that way, my lady,' Etta agreed. 'You were weary when you came off the barge, after the spell. Oh, my lady! It was wonderful – I've never felt so happy. You were right to do it, though no wonder it wore you out. But…' She swallowed again, and stepped back a little, as though she was scared Olivia might slap her.

'I won't be angry,' Olivia told her again. 'I need to know what happened.'

'People were talking, my lady,' Etta admitted slowly. 'They talk in front of servants as they never would to your face. They say your father, His Grace, I mean…' She hurriedly bobbed her knees in a little curtsey at his name.

'Yes, yes, my father,' Olivia said impatiently. 'What?'

'You took over the ceremony, my lady. And no one had said you would before. They're saying His Grace is sick.'

'Dying?' Olivia whispered.

'It was hinted,' Etta agreed reluctantly. 'And if he is, my lady, what if that's why you were so exhausted? That spell would wear anyone out. But I didn't want them to think you couldn't do it,' she went on, still eyeing Olivia cautiously. 'That seemed like it would be dangerous. If they thought you were only a little girl and not strong enough. *Please don't throw that!*'

Olivia looked down at the delicate painted ivory fan in her hands, and then up at Etta in surprise. 'I wasn't going to! I was just holding it...' But the thin ivory sticks had snapped, she saw now, because she had been gripping them so tightly. Her hand was bleeding a little, where one of the ivory splinters had driven into her skin. 'I really wasn't going to,' she murmured. 'Have I been that horrible to you, Etta? You were only telling me the truth.'

Etta was fussing over her hand now, wrapping a

lace-trimmed handkerchief around it to stop the blood dripping on to Olivia's dress, and then hurrying to send for hot water.

Olivia laughed. 'Oh! Coco! Look, Etta, he's peeping out – was he sleeping under that handkerchief?'

Etta looked down at her neat blue skirt, and tried to shoo the chocolate-coloured kitten back into the pocket of her best embroidered apron with her free hand. But he scrambled away from her, and clambered down her skirt, leaving a trail of little hooked threads.

'I hid him,' Etta explained, in between clucking anxiously at the kitten. 'I'm sorry, my lady, I can't catch him without letting go of this, and the blood dripping on your dress... I didn't trust him, to leave him here. I think the spell sent him to sleep, he was very good...'

Someone scratched on the door, and another maid appeared with the hot water.

'Oh, Etta, honestly, I can heal it,' Olivia murmured, looking down at the bloodstained handkerchief in distaste. 'I didn't think about it, that was stupid.'

'Not now, my lady. Not when you're so tired.' Etta looked down at her anxiously. 'And the sooner you can get back out there –' she nodded at the outer chambers, which were full of court ladies, Olivia could hear them chattering – 'the better. Don't you think, my lady? You don't want them talking. More than they are.'

'I need to show them I'm strong,' Olivia agreed slowly. 'You're very loyal, Etta, for someone I spend most of my time shouting at. Especially when you expect me to throw things at you.'

Etta only busied herself with binding up Olivia's hand. Her lips were pressed tightly together, as though she knew she had already said more than she should, and Olivia sighed, very faintly.

Her father wouldn't talk to her because he was too busy, and because he thought she was too young to understand, and to be burdened with the magic. *And perhaps because I'm a girl*, Olivia thought resentfully. She had never really wanted to be a boy – it would have meant weapons training, as well as all her other lessons. But she had a feeling that if she had been a prince, and not a princess, she might know a great deal more about what was going on. If she were the duke's *son*, she would have been trained in court politics, as well as how to use a sword. As it was, Olivia would inherit her father's magic, but she would still have to marry, and it would be her husband who would deal with the counsellors, and the ambassadors, and the navy.

Olivia would have her magic, and her children, and she would watch and listen while the men planned how to use her power. It didn't seem a very fair bargain. And already it meant that her father didn't talk to her about the important things. *Because he thinks it's too hard for a girl to understand!* Olivia growled to herself, and Etta glanced up at her worriedly.

She couldn't trust any of the ladies-in-waiting either, not for anything more than walking with her in the gardens, and gossiping and giggling and spying – both for her and against her. And she certainly couldn't trust her aunt.

Etta wouldn't talk to her, not properly, because she was only a maid, and she was too scared that Olivia might turn round and sack her, or maybe even have her thrown in prison. *Which I could, if I wanted, so I suppose she's right. And I did almost threaten to have her tortured, out there on the barge. It's my own fault she's not sure if she can trust me.*

I'll have to find someone else to ask. Someone who'll tell me what's going on in the city. Why that woman was so angry. What people think about Father dropping the ring. Someone I can trust. Perhaps even... Someone who doesn't know that I'm a princess? Olivia sighed. That was just ridiculous. She could go out in a mask, like at New Year, but not many people wore masks all the time. Only for grand parties, and for Carnival. A mask would mean that people noticed her *more*.

'There, my lady.' Etta smoothed the bandage, and pulled a needlebook out of another of her useful pockets. Olivia envied her those pockets very much, princess dresses did not come with pockets at all. Then Etta fetched a pair of deep lace cuffs from the wardrobe, and sewed them around Olivia's sleeves with tiny, neat stitches, so the lace ruffles fell over her hands, and the bandage was hidden.

All the time Etta sewed, Olivia stood watching her – her mouse-brown hair, smoothly drawn back into a knot, her fair, indoor skin, almost as pale as Olivia's own, reddened hands, from washing Olivia's delicate laces. Etta spent more time with her than anyone else, and still Olivia couldn't talk to her.

'I'm sorry,' she whispered, and Etta looked up at her in surprise, before quickly bowing her head again.

'I shouldn't have shouted at you, all the times I did. And thank you, for warning me about my aunt, and again just now. I think I trust you, Etta, even if you don't trust me.' She swallowed. 'And now we will go out there again.'

Etta nodded, and scooped up the kitten, who was trying to chase her apron strings. He wriggled, and ran out all his claws like tiny pins. She looked anxiously about the room, wondering what to do with him.

'Let's take him with us,' Olivia suggested. 'He can distract some of those stupid girls, and maybe someone will say something they shouldn't.' She glanced at Etta, and sighed. 'I know. Even the kitten gets mixed up in the court intrigue. It's horrible. Perhaps you should go home to your mother, Etta. It might be safer. No one plotting.'

Etta smiled at her. 'My mother works here in the

57

laundry, my lady. You'd be amazed at the amount she gets paid in bribes. Who wore what, and when.'

'Even the washing,' Olivia muttered. 'You can't keep anything secret. Oh, don't look at me like that! I've just not thought about it before, and you needn't smirk at the tiles. I was…busy.' *Doing lessons, and because of magic and etiquette and history, and not understanding what it was all for, and how soon I'd need it…*

CHAPTER THREE

'GOOD AFTERNOON, COUSIN.'

Olivia nodded politely to Zuan. She strongly suspected he always called her *cousin* so that he didn't have to say *my lady*. She didn't like him, but she knew that he hated her. If she hadn't been born, two years after him, he would be the duke's heir. A large number of the royal court thought he still should be. There hadn't been a duchess since Joanna, about two hundred years ago, and she had been a spineless, ill-tempered creature. Her husband's family had ruled Venice through her, and it was hinted in a lot of the histories that her sudden death had been the result of poisoning.

'Are you quite recovered?' Zuan asked smoothly, his eyebrows dipping together in a worried little frown. Everyone around them whispered how sweet he was, how concerned for his dear cousin.

'From what?' Olivia asked carelessly, flicking open her fan – a different one, with strong gold sticks, just in case. She kept her face innocently enquiring. She could feel so many people staring at her. Even those who weren't close enough to hear their conversation probably had charms out to catch a word here and there. Now that she was thinking about it, she could see the little wisps of magic, shimmering in the air. Probably most of them were accidental spells, just the gossipy court ladies wishing they could hear a little more, and mixing their thirst for news with a little unconscious magic. But her aunt was sure to have spells out here too.

Again Olivia wished it were fashionable to wear masks in the daytime, as well as for special evening parties. Then she could make horrible faces at Zuan and no one would know, not even Lady Sofia.

She was supposed to marry him, which just made her

want to laugh, most of the time. Except when she woke up in the middle of the night and worried that it might actually happen. No one could make her do it. Or at least she thought not. Lady Sofia might try, though. Even her father had indicated that it would be a tidy way of dealing with loose ends.

Olivia had always known that her marriage would have to be political. She was a princess, after all. She was a bargaining counter, a very valuable one. But surely she would have some say in it?

However good for the city it would be, she wasn't going to give in. She didn't believe the marriage would be that good for the city, anyway. Zuan was exactly the bully he looked, with his hulking shoulders, and small yellowish-golden eyes. And his magic was all about power too, there was no delicacy to him anywhere. She couldn't imagine him dealing with a foreign embassy, or planning some careful trading deal. He just liked hitting things and shouting at people. She shuddered a little, and then stiffened her spine furiously. What if he thought she was scared?

'You were ill, I thought? After the ceremony?

Wasn't that why you retired to your room?' He leaned a little closer, watching her hopefully. What was he expecting her to do, Olivia wondered. Keel over in the middle of the drawing room, and bequeath the duchy to him with her dying breath?

'Oh, no. My silly maid had left a loose thread on my dress, that was all.' She beamed at him sweetly. 'I have to be careful to be well-presented, you see. I do sometimes wish I could be like you, dear cousin. It must be wonderful to have no one care how you look.' She swept her gaze over his doublet, which was so heavily embroidered and jewelled that it creaked when he moved.

Zuan stepped back again as though she'd bitten him, and Olivia saw his top lip thin back a little over his teeth.

'Perhaps I was mistaken,' he muttered. 'So it was only your father who was taken ill.' He darted her a sharp sideways look.

Olivia drew in a little breath, and felt a hundred listening spells leap up and fasten on his words. *This* was what mattered.

'My father? His Grace the duke…' She watched carefully to see that Zuan dipped his head in respect, just as he should. 'His Grace the duke is quite well, Lord Zuan. Why would you think he was ill?'

Zuan forgot his careful court manners as far as to scowl at her. 'He collapsed!'

'He did not,' Olivia told him decidedly, lifting her head a little. If she had to, she was going to lie, and do it well. She could not let the court catch one little thread of doubt in her father's power, or they would worry him to shreds. She smiled sadly at Zuan, and let a little pinkness flush into her cheeks – she was furious, but her cousin could think that she was embarrassed, if he liked. 'My father kindly allowed me to take part in the spell with him. I had been begging him to let me for weeks.' She raised her voice. 'His Grace had warned me it was a strong enchantment, but I had no idea of the power it needed! I let the ring slip, so stupid of me. Fortunately, my father's magic was there to mend my mistake. It's lucky I have so many more years for him to guide me. His Grace held us all safe in his hands. Didn't he?'

Zuan stared back at her. It wasn't what he had seen,

and he knew it. So did Olivia, but she was willing to bet he wouldn't argue with her in front of everyone else.

'Didn't he?' she prompted, and her cousin nodded, and bowed.

'Indeed. My lady,' he added, forcing the words out between his crooked teeth.

Olivia felt the listening spells drop back a little, and the tide of whispers ran through the room again, as everyone tried to remember exactly what they had seen. Zuan bowed again, and stepped back. 'I promised my lady mother that I would…'

Report back, Olivia thought. *That's what you're trying not to say.*

'Wait upon her,' he finished stiffly. 'Good day, cousin.'

Even as they smiled and bowed, Olivia could almost see how much he hated her. It rolled off him in waves, like the stench of decay. If she were forced to marry him, she realised suddenly, he would make her life a misery, and mostly for the fun of it.

As Zuan clumped away in his high-heeled boots, Olivia felt herself sag a little. She was used to squabbling with him, but today there had been an extra layer of nastiness to their conversation. Deep down, Zuan had been so happy about her father's strange attack. It made her feel sick.

I shall have to go and talk to Father, Olivia thought to herself wearily, as she paced around her receiving room, smiling and nodding and trying to look as though she wasn't the slightest bit tired or worried. *I need to ask him what happened. We need to plan. I need to ask him if this is going to happen again. I can't ask him that! It's like I'm asking if he's dying…*

Is he dying?

Suddenly the smiling and the bowing and the twittering were just too much. She wanted to run away, but of course she couldn't. Everyone was looking, and besides, where would she run to?

She waved her hand imperiously at one of the page boys standing by the door, and he came running to kneel at her feet. 'Music,' she snapped. And then, remembering Etta, and her kindness, she added gently, 'Would you fetch the lute player, please?' She would have added the boy's name, but she couldn't remember it. There were a lot of servants, after all. Even so, the boy went red, and stammered, 'A-at once, my lady.' He practically ran out of the room. It was amazing what an effect being polite could have, Olivia thought guiltily.

As the lute player hurried into the room, Olivia sat down in the deep, cushioned window, and shushed the chattering girls who arranged themselves around her. 'I wish to listen to Signor Ferdi, and his beautiful music,' she said smiling.

The lute player went several shades paler. He wasn't really used to being listened to, and Olivia thought his fingers shook a little as he darted them across the strings. But now she had made it impossible for anyone to speak to her. Instead they would have to listen and smile, and as long as she looked like she was listening and smiling too, she could sit still and *think*.

Signor Ferdi was a very skilled lute player, even if he was more used to being background noise. His fingers scurried over the strings, and the music rippled out in waves. Olivia closed her eyes, and it seemed that she could hear the song in colours, each note jewelled and distinct. They spiralled away from her like a staircase, stretching out across the room, and it was too tempting not to walk out into the music.

Is this a spell? she thought to herself, as she felt some part of her begin to walk out into the room. *Has he bewitched me?* Part of her magical training – a large part – had been to protect herself against rogue magic (although strangely, no one had ever mentioned being enchanted by one's own aunt). This didn't feel like an attack. Perhaps it was just that she was so tired. Nothing like this had happened before, but it seemed easy to go travelling with the music away from herself. Olivia was almost sure that she could step back out of the song whenever she wanted. It was just...pretty. And useful, too... The music drifted out across the room, and Olivia drifted with it, coiling around the little murmuring groups, and listening.

Such a bad time for it to happen!

With all the flooding, you mean?

Well, it must be a bad omen, mustn't it, to have the ceremony disrupted like that. As though the duke isn't properly in control of the waters...

You mean his weakness is causing the floods? Oh no, you can't say that. Surely not.

Of course, I would never say that! But it does make one think…

Olivia swirled with the key change, and tore herself away. She was glad she was only hearing this with half her self. All of her might have wanted to slap the stupid young man, and that would only make everyone certain that he was right.

Riots in Venice…

Horrifying. I've never seen anything like it. Not just a few people, either, a huge crowd.

The taxes have gone up, and the price of bread is higher than ever.

But the taxes are to rebuild the flood defences, you'd think that people would understand, we can't leave the city open to the rising waters!

They shouldn't be rising, though, should they? Something's wrong.

Olivia broke away again, but it seemed that wherever the music took her, people were talking about flooding, and the spell, and riots.

She knew what riots were, of course, but she had never seen one. She had never even heard of one taking place in her city. The duke was known to be a fair ruler, kind, even, compared to some of his ancestors. His nickname was the angel, after all. Venice was happy, rich and contented, and so were its people. That was what she had always been taught. She didn't really *know*, of course. She only saw the city from a gondola, surrounded by guards. That old woman in the crowd this morning was the closest Olivia had come to one of her people in years.

If my father's magic is weakening, I shall need to help him like I did this morning, more and more often. But how can I, when he won't tell me what's happening? When he still thinks I'm a little girl? Even when I'm older, I'm just a girl who needs a husband to rule the city for her.

I need to find out what's happening in the city for myself. These riots – truly, in Venice? I have to know!

I could ask Etta, she thought, as Signor Ferdi drew his song to a close. *But I think she's still too frightened of me to tell me the truth.* She could feel herself settling back in as the music died away, and she looked up at

69

him and smiled. 'That was beautiful, Signor.'

No, Etta would just smile, and tell me it was nothing.

Besides, wouldn't it be more interesting to find out the truth for herself?

You shouldn't really be so excited about it, Olivia scolded herself, two days later, as she said goodnight to the lady-in-waiting who had been helping her practise her Talish conversation. Now there was only Etta, slipping about the room preparing her washing water, and her nightgown, and clucking at the faded flowers in her hair.

'It doesn't matter,' she murmured, trying to sound bored, and sleepy, when she had never felt so awake in her life. If only Etta would go! The ladies-in-waiting had their rooms next to Olivia's, but they were beyond her own little audience chamber. They were safely far away. No one would hear her. She twitched irritably under Etta's fingers as the girl uncoiled her dark wavy hair, and began to plait it loosely for the night.

'My lady?' Etta murmured anxiously.

'Nothing! Nothing! I have a headache, just a

little. Leave me, Etta, all I want to do is lie down.' She couldn't help glancing at her bed, and Etta nodded sympathetically, helping her out of the silken wrapper, and her little slippers. Etta was so gentle, and so kind that Olivia almost wanted to tell her that it was all right, she really wasn't ill. She hadn't been looking longingly at the linen sheets, and the feather pillows. She had been careless, and stupid – she had been looking at the bed because of what was hidden under it.

She lay there for a little while after Etta closed the door behind her – just in case the maid remembered a skirt not brushed, or a jewel not locked away – imagining that she could feel the box underneath the bed frame. It had been in her wardrobe room, a beautiful box, wood, but covered in a fine marbled paper. A dress must have been delivered in it once, or perhaps a fur.

She hadn't needed to hide the clothes, Olivia admitted to herself. But it had helped. It had made her feel as though she were doing something, planning. Stepping forward. The evening of the Wedding of the Sea, she had been so tired that her wrists shook as she undid the pearl drops from her ears. And then the night after, she had remembered that there was a concert in the Grand Audience Chamber, going on until late. Too busy, too many people coming and going, too many boats sliding quietly away on the dark canal. She had come upstairs and sat alone, fretting at a wisp of her hair. In the end she had got up and found the clothes, so at least she was doing *something*.

Tonight was the night.

Her fingers were shaking as she undid the shutter. She had never climbed out of her window before – but in a way, that made it easier. Olivia could tell herself that, anyway. No one would expect her to try to escape from the palace, because she was a princess, and she knew it. Princesses never climbed out of windows. And she had never been troublesome, in a hiding, climbing, running sort of way. Perhaps she would have been, had she had brothers and sisters. But it's hard to play hide and seek with one.

It was very sensible of princesses not to climb out of windows, Olivia decided, as she hung over the sill, looking down at the dark water. It wasn't all dark, though. There was light reflected in it from a hanging lamp high above, and the golden streaks shimmered on the water. That only made it look deeper and darker, and the way the lamp-gold swirled was a little bit sickening.

It would have been much easier to go out of a door, but there was at least one guard standing outside her chambers, and probably twenty more between there and the nearest outer door, which would be locked. So it was the window or nothing.

But at least the wall was thick, and old, and rough. It couldn't be all that hard to climb down. Then she would just have to edge along that narrow, foot-wide bit of bank till she could reach the street. She had magic to help, so it would be, well, not easy – but not impossible.

She had put her stoutest shoes on, and the plainest and least lacy of her petticoats. She hated going out dressed so immodestly, but she wasn't really planning for anyone to see her, and her outer dresses were all jewelled and showy, and impossible to climb down a wall in. The cloak was covered in the most beautiful embroidery, but it was black velvet and perfect for night-time. She just had to hope the embroidery wouldn't show at a passing glance.

Olivia pushed the shutters open a little wider, and bunched the petticoat up so she could swing her leg over the sill.

Really, she could just ask Etta about the riots. Or even her father! She looked down at the glittering, coldly swirling water again, and swallowed. She would actually rather climb out of a window above that water than go and talk to her father about exactly how his magic was failing him. She scrambled up on to the cold stone, and pulled at the fragile little cord that she had tied around her bed post. It looked thinner than ever, and she repeated the little spell she had added to strengthen the strips of her second-plainest petticoat that she'd tied together. The rope glowed, each fibre of the silk suddenly shining brighter, and she felt the strands thicken and catch her hands. It would hold. It felt friendly, even a little sticky, like the leftover stickiness after honey cakes.

It was with her mouth full of the remembered sweetness of honey that Olivia felt brave enough to climb out on to the wall. The darkness of the water sucked at her and her silly thin rope, but the honey held her hands tightly, and she edged downwards in the little gilded leather slippers that were the strongest shoes she had.

I'll climb down. And then I'll walk, she muttered to herself, over and over, as she crawled toe by toe down the stones. *Climb down, walk. Walk, and listen. Find the truth. This is my city. It will be*, she added hastily. *I have to know!*

The frightened face of the old woman suddenly appeared before Olivia's eyes, and she gasped. What had they done with her? She had looked angry, but frightened too – desperate, even. And she had been calling for the duke even as she was hurried away by the guards. Olivia's hands slipped on the cord as her spell slipped out of her mind, dislodged by the woman's sharp eyes and hollow cheeks. The leather soles of her shoes slid across the stones, and she gasped as her hand skidded and grazed on a sharp corner.

Then she fell.

It seemed to take a very long time. She hadn't been

that high up, but it felt as if she was falling for long enough to understand what was happening, and be frightened, and to try desperately to haul herself back with magic that didn't work. She was too full of falling, and not screaming, for magic. She couldn't pull the strands of the rope back together, or fly back up to the window, or even just stop still in the air and float. However hard she tried, she went on falling, until she hit the water, and fell on, deeper down.

CHAPTER FOUR

THE WATER FELT ODDLY THICK – thick enough to fight and thrash against. Olivia had never learned to swim – the canals were too dirty, and the lagoon was rough, and busy with ships. Only street urchins played in the water, even in the hottest of summers. This dark water felt nothing like Olivia's scented, steaming baths. It was hard to believe that this was the same stuff at all.

She flailed her arms, vaguely remembering the swimming children she had seen on her way to christen a new warship last summer. She had sailed past them in a gilded gondola, and they'd stared up at her, open-mouthed, struck dumb at the sight of the princess. But she had envied them, the coolness of the water, and the freedom to dive and splash and tear their ragged clothes even more. At least, she thought now that she envied them. Looking back, she seemed to remember being disgusted by so much grubby bare skin.

What had changed? she wondered dreamily as the bubbles of her own breath floated past her. What had turned her from a thoughtless, hard-hearted little princess, into someone who no longer threw things at her servants?

It couldn't only be Etta's surprising loyalty. It was fear, she supposed, rather sadly; a dark worry that had been growing inside her, ever since she had torn away her aunt's magic at New Year. One of her tutors liked to ramble on about fear, and how it changed history. She had never really understood him before. But there was the hole inside her now, a hole she didn't know how to close up. And every time someone looked at her sideways, or whispered about her father, the hole seemed to fill a little more of her, so that it was a great gaping emptiness, just under her ribs.

And then she gasped, and the emptiness was filled with water, and Olivia knew that she was drowning.

She fought, trying to drag herself back to the surface, but the water inside her weighed her down, and the dark velvet cloak wrapped itself around her arms. She felt her slippers sliding off her feet and reached out again, yanking at the jewelled fastening so that the cloak fell away. Then she tore desperately at the water, but now there was weed knotting around her fingers too. It grew along the length of the canals in great green ribbons, she had seen it. If she was tangled up in that, she would never get herself free. She kicked and dragged and tried to pull away, but she was stuck fast – except… she must have torn the clump of weed loose from its hold on the stones. It was rising up in the water, and it was pulling her with it. How could that be?

She was too grateful to care. She kicked again – she could see the glimmer of the lamplight on the water now. She was almost there!

As she came up to the surface, Olivia felt the tangle of the weed loosen from around her hands and stream away. She was pushed against the stone side of the canal with a soft bump, and the last tresses of weed stroked against her fingers.

She hung there, gasping, clinging to the stones and sucking in great lungfuls of air. That awful frightened hole inside her was gone for the moment, she was simply too glad to be alive.

And alive when she shouldn't be. The thought swam sluggishly into her head, and she peered out across the water, trying to see that strange, convenient clump of weed. She hadn't pulled it loose. It had loosened itself, and then it had pushed and pulled her back to the surface. She had felt it. True, she had been only half-conscious at the time, but still. It hadn't been weed; not just weed.

Impatiently she tried to flick her wet hair out of her eyes, but it wouldn't go, and she wasn't letting go of the bank to brush it away. She couldn't see clearly, but was that the waterweed? That whitish trailing thing under the surface?

Olivia gasped, and scrambled half out of the water with a strength she didn't know she had. The weed was looking at her, with dark, almond-shaped eyes.

'Careful, careful there,' the white thing muttered. 'That's it. Out of the water. Now, go on home. Silly child. More careful next time, do you hear? No, of course you don't,' it added, rather sadly, as it turned to swim away.

She watched it glide away, a long white shape cutting gracefully through the water. Bubbles foamed back from its strong shoulders, and what she had taken for weed was hair, she realised now. A mane... It was a horse! A swimming horse. A water horse, galloping away down the canal. As she watched, it snorted, and pounded the water into white spray with huge dark hooves. A faint memory stirred inside her, of a story someone had told her once. Her father? In one of his few visits to her nursery? She had been cuddled against an embroidered doublet, wriggling to avoid the sharp fleur-de-lis pattern digging into her cheek. It was all tied up together with the galloping hooves, splashing through the dark water. The water horses! She had begged him to carry her to the window, and show them to her. But her father had laughed and told her it was only a fairy story... There were no horses...

'I did hear you!' she called suddenly, surprising herself almost as much as she did the horse.

He looked back over his shoulder – she was sure the horse was a he, his voice had sounded male, deeper than her father's. Although perhaps all horses had deep voices, she thought wildly, as he turned and began to trot back towards her through the water. It was just that she had never known one to talk before, or swim, especially not under the water, as she was certain he had been.

He was bigger than an everyday horse, she decided faintly as he loomed over her, with water dripping off his long white mane. His mane had saved her, and she lifted one hand from her frantic grip on the cold stones, wanting to reach up and stroke it. She was not much accustomed to horses – the royal family used them rarely now, preferring to travel everywhere in the city by boat, or occasionally by sedan chair. The streets of Venice were too cramped and crowded for grand carriages.

'Careful,' he muttered again. 'Don't fall back in.' Then he looked at her sideways, bringing his great

head down close. 'Did you say something? Can you...
see me?'

Olivia nodded, and reached her hand a little closer.
Then she stopped, not sure if she should touch – but
she so wanted to. The pearly hair of his mane shone
in the darkness, glowing far brighter than the golden
lamps. She could still feel its springy pull against
her fingers. She had been stupid, thinking it was
waterweed. The horsehair was rough and strong, and
not the least bit slimy.

He lowered his head towards her a little, and she
could hear a shy, disbelieving happiness in his voice.
'You can touch me.'

Olivia ran her fingertips down the coarse hairs of
his mane, laughing as her own soft skin caught on the
damp roughness of the horsehair. She looked up at the
horse again, and saw that he was still gazing at her – as
though she was the strange one. Slowly, she moved her
hand from his mane to his head, and stroked the soft
warm velvet of his muzzle. He ducked his head, snorting
a bit, as though it tickled.

'Who are you?' he whispered, leaning down further,

and nudging against her wet hair. Then before she had time to answer, he nuzzled at her more urgently, and added, 'Child, you're so cold! Get a good hold of my mane, now. With both hands – do you trust me? Can you let go of the stones?'

Olivia nodded. She was cold – the excitement and fear of her fall, and then the rescue, were leaving her now. She was shaking, and her limbs felt heavy. Even though the horse was as soaked as she was, she could feel his warmth, and his mane seemed to wind around her like a blanket. Cautiously, she pulled her hand away from the stone edge of the canal, and wove her fingers into his white hair again. The great creature snorted approvingly, and plunged down into the water, so that with a squeak of fright she was dragged away from the bank and lifted on to his smooth, shining back.

So warm! Olivia leaned against his neck, torn by great, aching shivers, and she felt the horse's sides shake beneath her too, but only with laughter.

'What is it?' she whispered.

'We have old tales that tell of this,' he rumbled back,

84

between snorts of damp, horsey laughter. 'Humans who could understand us. And see us properly, not just as a glimpse under a bridge in the dead of night. I've dreamed of this for so long. A great magician! The deep, dark questions we would talk over. The grand themes. The poems and hymns we would use to celebrate each other.' He turned his head right round, and nudged her pale, cold cheek. 'And now I find you! A little soaked human child, too cold to talk to me, even though you can understand!'

'Are you d-d-disappointed?' Olivia stammered, through chattering teeth.

The horse snorted again, and his mane swirled round her, folding her in a warm white embrace. 'I suspect the great mysteries of life aren't as exciting as a good gallop through the midnight waters. Where have you come from, child? Who are you? And what were you doing in the middle of the canal, mmm?'

Olivia sighed. She was much warmer now, with his mane tucked round her, and his great bulk underneath. She had never ridden a horse, and she hadn't realised they were so…not exactly fat, but wide.

She felt a lot less drowned, and a little of her dignity was starting to come back. 'I fell out of the window,' she admitted reluctantly. 'Or off the wall, I suppose. I was climbing down.'

The horse looked up at the walls towering on either side of them. 'What, from up there? Are you mad?' He sniffed at her suspiciously again. 'What were you thinking? I don't deal in high up, I suppose. But even for a creature of the land like yourself, that looks most unwise.'

'It was,' Olivia muttered. 'I did have a rope, though. It's still there, look.' She pointed to her thin cord, fluttering from the window.

The horse eyed it, gave a disgusted sniff, and didn't say anything. Then he glanced at the buildings on either side of the canal again, and the Bridge of Sighs, arching overhead, and then at her, with a puzzled expression on his face.

Olivia fought the urge to giggle. Even she, who knew nothing about horses, could see that he was confused. He was looking at her sideways, and his ears were flickering.

'This is the palace, isn't it? And the prison, on the other side?'

Olivia nodded.

'Palace on that side, where your rope is?'

'Yes.'

The horse craned his head round, and gently nibbled one damp tress of Olivia's dark hair. She tried to sit still and look like royalty, even when the huge squarish yellow teeth were perilously close to her ear. He had rescued her, after all...

'A princess...' The horse drew back and stared at her. 'A princess, half-drowned in my canal?'

'How can you tell?' Olivia asked him curiously. 'Would I taste different, if I weren't royal?' She held back from telling him that actually, it was her canal. It seemed ungrateful.

'The old magic runs through you,' he murmured, looking away from her across the water. 'We've been part of the city for so long, and so have you. But everyone has forgotten us now, even your family, who were our closest companions, once.'

'Were we?' Olivia tried to lean round his neck, to get

him to look at her again. 'No one ever told me that! And you'd think they would have done, I'm supposed to know everything about our history. Because of having to rule, one day. It's meant to help.'

His head whipped round and he stared at her, his ears laid back in what looked like fright. 'You're the heir? You'll be the duchess?'

'Yes. I thought you knew – I'm the only child.'

'I thought you were a cousin, perhaps...' he muttered. 'We haven't watched your family closely, not for many hundreds of years. Since we grew apart. It was too sad. I should have known, though. I've seen you, oh, so many times, you and your father. But you look different.'

'I'm all wet!' Olivia pointed out. 'And I'm only wearing a petticoat.'

'True, true.' He flicked his mane away from her, and ducked his head. 'Why were you climbing out of the window, my lady?' he asked, his voice lower and softer than before.

'Please don't call me that,' Olivia said, without thinking. Then she added slowly, 'It was so nice...when you didn't know I was a princess. When you thought I was a silly little girl who'd fallen in the water.'

The horse's eyes strayed round to look at her, and his muzzle wrinkled in what she thought was probably a smile.

Olivia sniffed. She could see quite well what he was thinking. But his mane came creeping back around her, and the warmth was so good. 'The spell went wrong,' she said, still rather stiffly. 'I remembered something while I was doing it, and I was frightened and the rope failed. If it hadn't been for that, I wouldn't have fallen at all. And I was climbing out of the window for an important reason, not just to be silly.' It was hard to be dignified when she was still soaking wet, though, and her hair was straggling down the sides of her face, and dripping down her neck. The grand jewelled dresses she complained about so often did help her to feel more royal. 'My father is…not well. Do you watch the ceremonies? Did you know it was the Wedding of the Sea, two days ago?'

Another snorty laugh. 'I watched that great clumsy barge go lumbering out into the lagoon, yes.'

89

Olivia opened her mouth to argue, but then she decided that to a horse who could gallop through water, the barge probably did look stupid.

'I felt the magic,' the horse added. 'It was strong.'

Olivia went pink. 'I helped,' she said quietly. She shouldn't say, she knew. But it made her feel lighter, as if she were pouring away a little of her fear. And he had said that no one saw him. No one knew he was there. Who could he tell? 'I had to. He's supposed to do it by himself, but he couldn't! That's never, ever happened before. Everyone's whispering about it, and gossiping. There are so many rumours, and I don't know what's true and what isn't, and I can't ask anyone without making all the rumours more believable!' Without thinking, she yanked her clenched fists in his mane in frustration, and the horse gave a quiet whinny of protest.

'I'm sorry... I wanted to find out what was true. The court is – it's so stifling. I'm beginning to realise that I don't actually understand what's real, and what isn't.'

He was looking round at her doubtfully, and Olivia shook her head, wishing she could explain better.

'I don't ever see things that aren't perfect, don't you

90

understand? They repaint houses if Father or I are going past! And they do it to me too,' she added slowly. 'It works both ways. My aunt was setting spells on me, without me knowing. So that I was always sweet, and well-behaved and perfect. Nothing's *real*. People are talking about riots in the city, in my city, because the taxes have risen, and the price of bread is so high. I've never been hungry. I don't have the first idea what that could be like.'

'So you came to see…' the horse suggested.

'Yes. I was going to try to walk among the people, and hear what they really thought. And then, well, I suppose I was going to try to help. Somehow.'

'Good.' The horse nodded briskly. 'Come on, then.' And he turned, pulling away from the bank into the centre of the canal.

'Where are we going?' Olivia gasped, clutching his mane even tighter. She was curled sideways on his broad back, instead of riding astride, and she didn't feel very secure. The dark water foamed back along his sides as he plunged joyfully through – it was nothing like the smooth motion of a gondola.

'To find some people for you to talk to, of course! Now, ssshhh. A boat is coming. We'll draw in under the bridge.'

Olivia took in a shuddering breath of relief as he darted into the dark pool of shadow under a small bridge. Once he had stopped, she wriggled herself round so that she was sitting with one leg on either side of him. She didn't care if it was unladylike, or that it was uncomfortable. It felt a great deal safer. 'Can't they see us?' she whispered, as a gondola went softly past, the only sound the slow dipping of the oar. There were at least two people inside, she could see them, dark shapes huddled together inside the cave-like *felze*.

'No,' the horse breathed back. 'They aren't looking, even the gondolier. No one sees us.'

'I did.'

He nuzzled her gently. 'Indeed you did. I still don't know how.'

'Maybe it was because you rescued me? Although I did think you were a clump of waterweed, to start off with.'

He snorted a laugh. 'Waterweed. A piece of floating

rubbish. A lucky eddy in the water. There's always something. No one sees us water horses, when we push them back up to the surface.'

Olivia hugged his neck tighter. 'There are *more* of you? A whole herd of water horses?'

'Not as many as there used to be.' He gave her a thoughtful, sideways look from one dark eye. 'We need a lot of magic, I think. The city's power isn't as strong these days. It's still there, in the water, and the stones, but it doesn't sing to us, the way it did once. The magic was everywhere, in all of you...a long time ago.'

Olivia felt cold again, and her fingers fumbled in his mane. 'You think the rumours are true, then? It isn't just that Father is getting weaker – it's the whole city! That's why everything is going wrong? The waters are rising, and the people are angry?'

'Hmf.' The horse shrugged, she felt it, like a great ripple of weariness heaving through him from nose to tail. 'Maybe.'

'You don't seem all that worried!' Olivia snapped.

He sighed, and nosed his way out into the deeper water again. 'Long ago, dear child, I would have been.

But no human has spoken to us in so long, don't you see? And the magic is thinner, and rarer, and I am weaker. I sleep more than I did once. Everything inside me seems slower than it used to be, even my fears. We try to hold the waters back for you, but it's hard, without the magic behind us. The more you all forget, the weaker we are.'

His head was hanging a little, and his striding canter through the water had slowed to a shambling trot. Olivia laid her cheek against the muscles of his neck. 'I'm sorry. Did rescuing me tire you out? You don't seem weak at all, you know.' Then she added, half-whispering from a shyness she had never felt before, 'You're the most beautiful thing I've ever seen. I can't believe I'm riding you.'

'Ha!' The horse lifted his head, and shook his mane back proudly. 'As beautiful as my statue?' he asked, his voice light, as though he didn't really care what she answered.

'Oh! They're you!' Olivia seized his forelock, and pulled his head around, running her hand over his bony forehead, and the beautiful hollows of his eyes. How

94

could she not have seen it? 'The horses in the square are you… No one ever told me that. My tutor said they were probably from some old statue of a king in a chariot! Which one is you?'

'The rightmost.' He snorted smugly, and turned back to the water with a flick of his forelock. 'If you're looking up at us, I mean. The other three are my brothers. But they cropped our manes, of course. The sculptor refused to try to make them. The poor man cried, when he saw me up close.'

'But – they're hundreds and hundreds of years old,' Olivia murmured. 'They've been there for ever, practically.'

'And so have we.' The pride drained out of his voice, and he only sounded sad. 'Like I told you, child. We've always been here, part of the city. But you forgot about us.'

'I won't forget,' Olivia promised him. Then she added anxiously, 'I won't, will I? It won't be like a dream, that I forget when I wake up? I've had odd dreams before, even dreams that felt like magic, and then they slipped away.'

Olivia clutched at the water horse's mane again, and it coiled lovingly around her fingers. 'This *is* real. It's happening now, it isn't just a dream. I can't forget you. I won't. I refuse,' she added, in her most princessy voice. 'So you had better take me to find these people to talk to, so we can get on with mending…everything.'

CHAPTER FIVE

'WHAT IS YOUR NAME?' Olivia asked suddenly, as they turned into one of the smaller side canals, heading deeper into the city, away from the lagoon, and the palace.

The horse flicked his great white tail, and foam splashed up behind them. 'Lucian,' he told her proudly. 'And you, my lady?'

'Olivia.'

'Olivia,' he said thoughtfully. 'Princess Olivia...' He was silent for a moment, and then he added, 'A very grand name. I think you had better not think of yourself as *Princess Olivia* for the rest of the night. It will be easier to go spying if you're not a princess.'

'I'm not spying!' Olivia protested, rather faintly. She wasn't sure how to argue with a magical creature. Maybe he would simply disappear if she contradicted him.

'What would you call it, then?' Lucian asked, flicking his mane.

'Princesses don't spy...' Olivia said stubbornly. 'I'm...gathering intelligence.'

'Whatever you want to call it. But you can't do it thinking of yourself as Princess Olivia. Someone will end up slapping you.'

'They wouldn't dare!' Lucian sighed, and Olivia leaned close against his neck again. 'I see what you mean,' she admitted quietly. 'Very well. I'll try.'

'Start with your name,' Lucian advised. 'Not Olivia. Livi.'

No one had ever called her that. It sounded completely different. She whispered it to herself, trying out the sounds. 'Livi. Livi...'

'A young girl who works at the palace, perhaps,'

Lucian suggested. 'You should know enough about it to be convincing.'

Olivia laughed. 'I could be my own maid.' She looked down at her sodden petticoat. Even though it was filthy with mud and weed, it was still clearly lace-edged. 'Do you think this is too grand? I could always say it was a hand-me-down from myself.'

'Ssshhh… We're here,' the water horse murmured. 'The Bridge of the Smiling Fishes.'

'The what?' Olivia hissed back, suddenly realising that she had never seen this bridge before. She had never even been down this rather shabby little waterway. She had thought the city belonged to her, but she only knew the Grand Canal, and a few others she was escorted along to visit a church, or to watch a ceremony. It wasn't her city at all… She shook her shoulders, and sat up straighter. She would *make* it hers. 'What did you say it was called?' she whispered again.

'Bridge of the Smiling Fishes. The carvings. You may not be able to see in the dark.'

'Oh…' Olivia peered at the stonework as they came closer, but he was right, all she could see were the faint shadows around the carved decoration. 'Why this bridge?'

'Underneath.' Lucian glided slowly up towards the bridge, and Olivia saw that there were walls around its base – it had been built with heavy stone blocks that jutted out from the bank, so that underneath its deep arch there was a flat, dry space. Now her eyes were adjusting to the gloom under the arch, she could see that the stones were covered in small, ragged bodies, all huddled together for warmth.

'Children!' she whispered to him, shocked.

'Yes. Here, climb off my back. Just here look, next to the bridge. Tell them you fell in, and you've just managed to climb out. Ask where you are. Good luck, little princess. I'll stay back here.'

'Thank you.' Olivia scrambled clumsily off his back and on to the pavement just along from the bridge, shivering as her bare feet met cold stone. She turned to watch as he swirled around and sank under the water again, so only a faint shimmer of white showed where he waited. She thought of the burning in her chest when she sank like that, and then the water rushing in to fill that fearful gap. Could Lucian breathe underwater?

'Who are you? Get out of it. No room.'

Olivia gasped, and turned. The children under the bridge had been watching her, while she stood there daydreaming.

'Find somewhere else to sleep!' One of the bundles of rags undid itself and stood up, turning into a boy, smaller than Olivia.

'I d-don't want to sleep here,' she answered, trying to tell herself that she was stuttering with the cold, and not because she was frightened of this rough-looking creature. Her own hair was probably just as straggly as his by now. *But I don't smell like that.* She cast the thought away, and tried to beg. 'I fell in the water. I don't know where I am. Can't I just sit here a minute, and catch my breath?'

'No.'

Olivia gaped at him, not quite sure what to say. She wasn't used to people saying no to her. Even if she had only been an everyday girl, not a princess who was used to instant obedience, that seemed like a perfectly reasonable request, to her. Why couldn't she sit down? She dug her nails into her palms to stop herself snapping, and realised she was feeling better. Being a little bit angry was good. *But you don't want to be slapped*, she reminded herself.

'I can't just go,' she explained beseechingly, trying to widen her eyes, like one of the ladies-in-waiting she disliked most intensely, a silly, fluffy-haired girl who could always get people to do whatever she wanted. 'I really don't know where I am. Can't you tell me how to get back to the palace?'

'The palace?' Another ragged heap shifted and sat up. 'Jac, look at her. She's got lace on that dress. She's not one of the bridge children, she's got family. Money, probably. She'll send someone after us. Get up, all of you!' And the girl – despite her hoarse, cracked voice, Olivia was sure it was a girl – started to shake the others, hissing, 'Get up, get up, all of you, we've got to move on.'

'Oh, no, you don't, please!' Olivia gave up on begging with words, and threw all her magic into it instead, sending out little silken bindings to tie the ragged children to her and stop them hurrying away. She thrust away the thought that she was behaving like her aunt – she had good reasons, didn't she?

'You stop that!' the boy snapped. 'No spells round here. You'll be getting us all in trouble.' And he caught her bindings, snarled them into a knot and cast them back at her. The magic wriggled along the stone pavement in a squirming bundle, like a shamed dog, until it coiled itself gratefully around Olivia's toes, and sank back in.

'How did you do that?' Olivia asked, entirely forgetting her mission now. She was usually very good at spells for obedience, partly because she was so practised at ordering people around anyway. 'I've never seen anyone do that before.'

'Don't know, don't care. Out. And take that great white thing you've got with you too. You never fell in the water, little liar. I saw him set you down.'

Olivia gasped. 'You can see him? *And* you ripped up my spell! Are you a magician?'

The boy rolled his eyes at her. 'Looks like it, don't it, little miss, living under a bridge? Go away!' But then his eyes widened, and Olivia turned to see what he had seen, and gasped. Lucian was rearing out of the water just behind them, his great hind hooves planted just below the surface of the water, and his white mane and tail coiling in a froth of foam and bubbles. His nostrils were flared and red with excitement, and his eyes glittered as he loomed over the children like a ghost horse.

'I thought it was a dog...' the boy muttered, wild-eyed, as he staggered back against the underside of the bridge.

'You shouldn't be able to see him!' Olivia gasped. But all the children could, it was clear – they were terrified, and one of the smallest ones was screaming over and over with her mouth pressed into her ragged sleeve. Somehow that was the worst thing – the tiny girl couldn't even let herself be properly scared, in case someone caught them.

'He's not a monster,' Olivia cried, running to the edge of the bank and reaching out to Lucian. 'He won't hurt you, he's happy. He's surprised! Aren't you?' she added fiercely to the water horse. 'And get down!'

Lucian subsided into the water with a crash, and ducked his head guiltily. 'My apologies, my lady. Livi,' he corrected himself quickly. 'But all of you! In one night!' His mane was coiling and uncoiling itself like a nest of snakes, and Olivia could see why the bridge children were still cowering back against the stones.

'You're frightening them,' she whispered. 'Keep still. And can't you look smaller?'

The huge horse stamped his hooves, and circled, and tried to settle lower in the water, till at last he was submerged to his shoulders, as he had been when Olivia first saw him – but his mane was still dancing.

'What is he?' croaked the boy. *Jac*, the others had called him.

'A water horse… I wasn't lying before,' Olivia said slowly, trying to think how much to tell them. 'I did fall in, and he rescued me. That's what they do, but for years, no one's been able to see. And then I did, just tonight, and now you're seeing him, and you can hear him too, that's why he jumped out of the water like that. He was excited. Are you sure you aren't magicians?'

'It can only be because they live so close to the water,'

Lucian said, paddling closer, and sniffing eagerly at the littlest girl. She had stopped screaming by now, she just gazed at him, her eyes night black in a pale smudge of face. 'No court ritual. No history. No training. Just magic. They're like the first people of your city, building their lives out of the marshland. The water belongs to them.'

Jac eyed him suspiciously. 'It does,' he agreed. 'That's all we've got. There are more of you, she says? I've seen you before. Thought I was seeing things. When the flood came with that big storm, months back – you were all charging up on the tide.'

Lucian nodded. 'To hold back the waters. That's what we do – we protect the city, and guard the water. And the people.' He nuzzled at the little girl who'd screamed, and she squeaked, and then laughed, sounding almost surprised at herself. 'Don't you remember, little thing?'

'He pushed me back out…' she whispered. 'When the water was so high that time. We were all close to the edge. Anna rolled on me, and I was asleep, and I fell in. He pushed me out again.'

The older girl stared. 'That morning when you were all wet,' she whispered. 'I never believed you…' She turned and frowned at Olivia. 'So who are you?' she demanded. 'You fell in, and he rescued you. Why didn't he just take you home? What did he bring you here for?'

'I fell in while I was out on an errand,' Olivia explained, thinking it out as she went. Most of the story they'd thought up would still work, wouldn't it? 'For my mistress. I'm a maid to the princess. I was hurrying, and I slipped.'

'Her dress is nice enough for someone who works in the palace,' one of the other girls remarked. 'It's like a princess dress. Look at the little flowers.'

Olivia smoothed the battered petticoat, and tried not to smile. 'Princess Olivia sent me to find people and talk to them. Everyday people, not from the court. She's sick of only hearing whispers from her ladies-in-waiting.'

'Whispers about what?' Jac asked.

Olivia swallowed. Now that she was here, at last, doing what she had set out to do at the beginning of this strange long night, she was almost too frightened to ask.

'My – I mean, the duke. Have you heard anything about him?'

'Like what?'

'We know he's dying,' the littlest girl chirped, patting Lucian's nose, and looking up at Olivia as though she hoped she was being helpful.

Olivia stared at her, and then round at the others, but none of the other children shushed the little one, or told her not to be stupid. As far as they could see, obviously, the baby had only spoken the truth.

She swallowed painfully. 'He's not dying,' she forced out in a whisper.

'He is.' Jac folded his arms, and nodded firmly. 'Everyone says so. That's why the floods are getting worse. There never used to be floods this time of year, did there? Floods are a winter thing. We know – we got summer places and winter places. Higher up in the winter, you see? To keep out of the high water. Now we don't use the low ones even in the summer. Can't risk it. Besides, the water feels different. Wilder. Like the magic's too weak to hold it all in place.'

'Oh.' Olivia nodded. He sounded so certain.

'And that's because of the duke?'

'Course. His magic holds everything together, don't it? So if things are falling apart, that's why. Your princess, is she strong?'

Olivia opened her mouth, but she couldn't answer.

'Yes.' Lucian looked around at them all, and his voice was deep and fierce. 'She will be. Strong enough to mend it all. I know magic, and hers is true. She's a child of the water, just like you.'

The oldest girl gave a little shrug and glared at Olivia. 'You tell her to hold the waters back, then, and give us somewhere dry to sleep again.'

'I will,' Olivia promised shakily. 'I could come back and bring you some food,' she offered. 'If I tell the princess, she'll let me.' She wasn't quite sure how she was going to get back into the palace tonight, let alone out again another night, but she knew that she would, somehow. She couldn't go back to lessons, and court manners, and never touching the water now. She would bundle up her ragged petticoat and hide it for another night, and she would come back.

CHAPTER SIX

'MY LADY? MY LADY, WAKE UP!'

Etta was definitely not whispering, Olivia thought, in surprise. That was not her polite, well-trained servant's whisper at all.

But then, she wasn't tucking her head underneath her pillow and pretending that Etta wasn't there just to be troublesome. She actually was exhausted. All that extra magic last night, making the rope, and then the almost-drowning, and the legendary-water-horse-meeting, and the talking to commoners for the first time ever... She had a right to be tired.

'Oh, my lady, please... Here, little one, you wake her.'

Olivia pulled her head out from under the pillow. That wasn't just Etta in a hurry to get her into the latest torturous jewelled dress. There was an edge of panic in her maid's voice, Olivia recognised it. She had spent a lot of the last night feeling just the same.

Then she giggled, without meaning to at all. Something was padding slowly and determinedly across her back, something with very small feet.

'Very clever, Etta,' she said, wriggling round and scooping the kitten up in her cupped hands. 'Good morning, little sweetness.' The kitten was squirming, eager to be off exploring the interesting hollows of the counterpane. Olivia smoothed one hand over his silky chocolate fur – so much softer than a mane – and let him go, laughing as he clambered up the hill of her knees.

'My lady...'

Olivia turned to stare at Etta in amazement. The girl had touched her! She had laid her hand on Olivia's fingers. Etta *never* touched her, not unless

111

she was fastening a dress, or braiding her hair.

'I'm sorry, my lady.' Etta stepped back with a gasp. 'I forgot myself. But your father is ill...'

Olivia caught the kitten again, lifting him off his triumphant pose on top of her knees, so that he squawked indignantly. She stuffed him into Etta's hands, and threw back the bedclothes. 'How ill?' she demanded. 'And who knows? Help me dress, now.'

'Everyone knows,' Etta murmured miserably, setting the kitten on the window seat and fetching Olivia's washing water. 'Everyone is talking about it. He was taken ill in the night. All the audiences for today have been cancelled. And the waters are rising, my lady. Some houses are flooded already.'

'Then he really must be ill,' Olivia murmured anxiously. 'Etta, who is in charge, if my father is confined to his bed?' She knew it was stupid to have to ask her maid, but it was a question that had never been covered in her lessons.

'The Council of Ten, I suppose.' Etta shivered. The council were almost as powerful as the duke, and the whole city feared them.

'Of course. And that means my aunt. They will never be able to stand up against her, none of them. Especially since she persuaded Father to put Zuan on the council too, when he turned fourteen. All he does is parrot what she tells him. Find me a sober sort of dress, Etta. But something that makes me look taller. I know Lady Sofia. She will be telling everyone I'm too young to be consulted about anything, I know it.'

'The green silk, my lady?' Etta hurried out of the wardrobe, with a dark green dress over her arm.

'Ye-es.' Olivia frowned at it. 'Does it make me look tall?'

Etta opened her mouth, shut it again, and then said firmly, 'Yes, my lady.'

'I know you're lying, but thank you, Etta.'

The duke's chambers were frighteningly quiet, Olivia thought, and she walked a little faster, her heels tapping sharply on the marble floors. Usually, messengers were scurrying in and out, and there would be petitioners waiting outside, hoping to be admitted to the duke's presence. They would wait for hours, all night sometimes. It was odd – wrong, almost – to see the great doorway empty, except for a guardsman.

The soldier was watching out of the corner of his eye as Olivia approached, with Etta pacing behind her, and Coco some way behind Etta, because he kept darting off to explore and then had to hurry to catch up.

If he dares to tell me that I can't go in, Olivia thought, *I'll…what?*

She didn't know. Could she order the guard to let her in? What could she threaten him with? She would be a duchess one day, but at this moment, she had no power of her own. All she could do was look down her nose, and hope that was enough, that everyone would remember who was to come after the duke.

She stopped by the guardsman, and stared at him meaningfully. He swallowed, and looked at his boots, and then he opened the door. Olivia was almost sure that he had been told not to, he had that look about him, of someone forced to choose the lesser evil.

And you're right, she told him silently as she stalked on by. *Whatever my aunt threatened you with, I could be a hundred times worse. I could.* But then she looked back at his worried face, his eyes gleaming with fright under the shadow of his helmet, and smiled at him.

'He'll be glad to see you, my lady,' the soldier gabbled. And then he stared straight ahead, as if he hadn't said anything, and as if he didn't know there was a small brown kitten climbing up his left boot.

Olivia elbowed Etta, who snatched the kitten up and tucked him into her apron, and they sailed away across the huge receiving room, which was empty, apart from a nervous huddle of alchemists and physicians close to the door of the inner chamber. Everyone else had gone. Had they given him up for dead already? Olivia thought bitterly as she stalked over to the doctors.

They were holding a jar of something unpleasant up to the light of the window, and they didn't dare to stop her either. They just bowed deeply, so deeply that Etta had to grab the one holding the jar before it went everywhere.

'Is my father awake?' Olivia demanded of the oldest and grandest-looking of the physicians.

'I'm afraid not, my lady. He is...weary.'

115

'Is that all?'

They gazed back at her silently, until one of the other doctors, a magician she recognised, from when she'd had a fever a year before, stepped forward.

'My lady, we're not sure what is wrong with the duke. He is not an old man – not so very old, but he is worn out, and frail. He hardly has the strength to sit up. He summoned Dottore Francisco, here, with a spell, last night, when a spasm overtook him. And that spell seemed to use up the last of him.'

Olivia nodded, a stiff little gesture that was all she could manage. He seemed to understand, and went on, his voice very soft.

'We cannot cure him, my lady. No one can. He simply needs to rest.'

He needs not to have the weight of the city on his shoulders, Olivia thought, but she dared not say it, and the physicians certainly would not, even though they all knew the truth. The words would be treason, if they were spoken aloud, and someone in that little huddle of learned men would run with them to the council, or Lady Sofia, or some other spymaster.

Olivia turned away, and a sleepy page opened the inner door for her, ushering her into the dim, airless space where her father lay.

The room was full of candles, but all they did was make the shadows darker. Olivia crept through the ornate furnishings, trying not to stumble in the eerie gloom. Her father's bed was even larger than her own, a great curtained gilded thing that made the wasted figure propped against the pillows just seem frailer. Olivia was used to meeting him in rich embroidered clothes, and a cap adorned with curling feathers. It frightened her to see that he was so small. She climbed up the little painted steps, and lay next to him on the purple silken bedspread, her hand over his own cold one. It reminded her of being small again – he hadn't held her in his arms for so long.

'Why didn't you call me, last night?' she whispered. 'Perhaps I could have helped? Or maybe you didn't want me to… Is it that you're too proud to ask? I can't believe that… Did you not see that your strength was failing? Oh, why am I only here now, when you can't talk to me? And what am I to do about Lady Sofia?'

The chill fingers twitched under her own, and Olivia felt the faintest stirring of her father's magic. It had always been their way to talk to each other, that sense that the other was close by and safe. But now she wished they hadn't shared that closeness – without it they might have spoken to each other properly instead, knowing that it was the only way they could. She might know now what she needed to do.

Olivia... The voice in her head was thread-like, hardly there at all.

'Don't,' she said firmly. 'Dottore Francisco said you must rest. In a few days...' She swallowed, and went on more firmly, 'In a few days you will be well again, and the waters will fall. I know it.'

She didn't, and she thought her father probably didn't either. But saying the words out loud gave her a sense of determination, and strength. The strength she needed for where she had to go next.

The Council of Ten met in a small, nondescript sort of room, dark with wood panelling – as nondescript as any room in such a palace could be. Olivia thought that they would summon her quite soon, but she didn't intend to wait and be sent for. It would be far better to present herself to the council unexpected, and not as a troublesome child hauled before her elders.

The young clerk sitting at the table piled with papers in the anteroom was probably writing the summons when they arrived, Olivia decided. When a kitten pounced on his quill pen, and he glanced up in annoyance to find the princess tapping her foot in front of him, he looked quite shocked. His mouth fell open, and he didn't get up.

'This is your princess,' Etta hissed at him disgustedly, and he scrambled out of his chair at once to bow.

'Announce me,' Olivia ordered, when he was still half stooped over.

'Oh!' He straightened up, and tried to put his cap back on. 'My lady, I can't, they're not supposed to be disturbed... I suppose... I mean...' He faltered into silence as Olivia glared at him. 'Yes, my lady...'

'Announce me, *now*.'

He gave up struggling with his cap, and twisted it between his hands instead as he led them to the door, opened it, and said miserably, 'The Princess Olivia.' Then he scuttled out of the way and slammed the door behind her, before anyone could blame him for her sudden arrival.

This dress makes me look tall, Olivia repeated to herself, as she paced slowly around the council table to the gilded wooden chair at the end – her father's seat.

She paused beside it, and looked thoughtfully at the places around the table. The nine other chairs were all taken.

'Cousin.' She nodded at Zuan. 'Will you be so kind as to move this chair for me? I cannot sit in my father's seat, but I wish to stand in his place, while he is…away.'

Zuan darted a glance at his mother, but she said nothing. He got up and shoved the golden chair away, so that it shrieked across the stone floor.

'Good morning, my lords. My lady.' Olivia nodded politely at the members of the council, who were staring back at her – some with interest, and some with obvious irritation. It had been a good idea to stay standing. Sitting down, she would be even smaller.

120

'I apologise for not being here before. I have been visiting my father.'

Several members of the council fidgeted a little, as though their chairs were uncomfortable.

'How is my dear brother?' Lady Sofia leaned forward, her eyes dark with sympathy and concern.

Olivia smiled thinly, and refused to look at her aunt for more than a second. 'He is very tired, my lady. It seems to me that battling the rising floodwaters has drained his strength. It will be the duty of the council to support him in this great task, of course.'

A hissing ran round the room, and a rustling of gowns, as the councillors leaned closer to each other to whisper. In theory, all the greater members of the court were magicians, it had always been so. But over the last few years, even the great families, those who had supported the dukes throughout the centuries in their care for the city, had begun to lose their magic.

'We were discussing the situation, in fact, before you came to join us,' Lady Sofia went on sweetly. 'The safety of the city is most important, of course.'

'The city and the people,' Olivia put in, thinking

of Jac, and that tiny little child who had rolled into the floodwater.

'Indeed.'

Olivia could feel her aunt gently twisting magic around her, just as she herself had tried to do with Jac. Unfortunately, Olivia couldn't rip the spell up and fling it at Lady Sofia, satisfying though it would be. Instead she smiled, and stroked the pendant hanging around her neck. It was a jewel her father had given her, a tiny enamel carnival mask. It was practically worthless next to the great jewels she wore for state occasions, but that only made it dearer. She had enchanted the dark amethysts set in the eyeholes of the mask a little while after he had first given it to her. It was a protection spell she had found in one of her tutor's books. Back then, she hadn't expected to need protecting, not with her father's strength there to guard her, not before she knew how her aunt had wrapped her round with magic and used her like a puppet. It had been an experiment, nothing more. But now she was glad of it. She needed her wits about her for facing the council, she couldn't protect herself against Lady

Sofia and think at the same time. The amethyst eyes burned cold under her fingers, and the spell misted out around her in a bright shield. Lady Sofia's magic crawled around it irritably, banging up against the shield like little buzzing flies, and Olivia saw her forehead pinch into a frown.

Her aunt's voice was louder when she spoke again. 'We must face the fact, my child, that your father will not live for ever.' She raised a hand to still the flurry of horrified whispers. 'I have every confidence that he will recover from this attack, but sooner or later, you will be the duchess. And I think your father would agree with me that it is much harder to rule alone.' She dropped her head, and sighed dramatically. Zuan glared at Olivia, as though it was her fault his mother was so upset, and patted her hand carefully. Lady Sofia lifted her eyes bravely, and went on in a shaking voice, 'Even guarding our family estates for the last two years without my dear husband, the father of my children, has been a terrible strain on me. You, my dear, will need a husband to support you in your reign.'

Take over my reign, you mean, Olivia thought,

watching the way that Lady Sofia couldn't resist glancing at Zuan.

Her cousin smirked at her. He was so disgustingly smug.

Marrying Zuan was one of those things that had been talked about since Olivia was born. On days when she hadn't actually had to see her cousin, it had seemed as though it might be bearable. But at that moment, it became perfectly clear to Olivia that she could not do it. She would not.

As soon as her father was better, she would explain to him, once and for all. She was quite sure that he'd support her, even if he were disappointed. She just had to avoid being formally promised to Zuan in the meantime.

She smiled sweetly at her aunt, and her cousin. 'I cannot possibly consider marriage with Father so ill. Besides, I think we should be concentrating on the floods, not a betrothal party.'

One of the elderly men at the other end of the table leaned forward. Lord Matteo. Olivia wondered if he had troublesome daughters – he seemed to be eyeing her with dislike. Was it just because she was a girl? 'Your marriage is not just about *you*, princess. We must give the people something to distract them from the flooding. A day of happiness. Revels. Grants of food to the poor, to show your love and mercy for the city.'

'You want my betrothal to be a distraction?' Olivia asked, widening her eyes and trying to look shocked. 'The marriage of your future duchess? Surely a little more thought needs to go into it than that, Lord Matteo?'

Someone sniggered, and Olivia tried not to look triumphant. She couldn't afford to make any enemies. 'But I agree with you, sir,' she went on. 'The people are suffering. Could we not give gifts of food for some other reason? To celebrate the Wedding of the Sea, perhaps?'

The old lord humphed, and settled grumpily back in his seat, but at least the council seemed to have forgotten the tricky problem of her marriage. The various lords squabbled over where the money for grants of food should come from – or more accurately, where it shouldn't, as each of them fought to protect his own department. When the ornate griffin-clock set into the centre of the table raised its wings and shrieked to tell the hour, the lords shuffled away, still arguing, and Olivia was left with her aunt and her cousin.

'Olivia, are you angry with me, dearest?' Lady Sofia purred. 'You seem…distant.'

'Only very worried about Father, dear aunt.' Olivia darted across to kiss Lady Sofia's scented cheek, and then made for the door before she could be held – she wasn't sure how well her shield would work if she was forced too close.

It still seemed odd to be thinking such things. She had no memory of her mother, and for years her aunt had been a sort of substitute, even if she wasn't a very good one. It hurt that all those cosy discussions about dresses, and the lessons in etiquette and deportment and fan-waving and the royal families of Europe had not been for her at all, Olivia thought, gulping painfully. She had always known that her aunt wanted her to marry Zuan, but it seemed so much clearer now. All those sweet kisses, and fragrant embraces from her loving aunt – they had all been about Zuan, and his chance to steal the throne.

My loving aunt would poison me quite happily, Olivia decided, as she walked back to her rooms. *In a few years' time, when I'd borne a son to carry on the family line – or perhaps two, just in case. Anyway, after that, I expect I might have an unfortunate accident.*

CHAPTER SEVEN

OLIVIA LAID THE DOLL IN the centre of her bed, leaning artistically sideways against the pillows. It had dark hair and eyes like her own, which would make the spell easier. She was determined that this expedition out of the palace would go more smoothly than the last one, and she had spent the last two days hidden away in her father's rooms, making sure that it would.

The duke's chambers were the only place she felt safe from Lady Sofia and the council. Her aunt seemed to have realised finally that Olivia was old enough to know her own mind, and that she was avoiding the sweetening spells that had been laid on her for years. Olivia could feel that Lady Sofia was watching her, all the time, and planning. She had tried to suggest that Olivia should attend her lessons, or walk in the courtyard for fresh air, but Olivia had told her sadly that she was worried for her father, and wished to spend as much time with him as she could. Which was true, of course. It just wasn't the only reason she wanted to stay with him.

She had returned to her father's chambers two days before, after the council meeting, dismissed the physicians hovering around him, and curled up on the bed by his feet. Quietly, she had started to tell him about the council meeting, about her growing fear of her aunt and her cousin, and her worries about the council, scheming and squabbling to gain as much power as they could while he was unconscious.

Olivia hadn't thought that her father could hear her. She was talking as much for herself as she was for him, trying to puzzle out what she should do. But when she told him about Lord Matteo, and her guess that he didn't much like his own daughters, she had heard her father laugh, but not out loud. It had been the faintest breath of amusement, that was all, and she had felt it through his magic.

'Are you awake?' she whispered hopefully.

His eyelids fluttered, and his mouth twitched a little in the smallest smile. 'Almost…' he whispered, and then his eyes opened, just a slit of their darkness showing. 'Olivia, I can't protect you as I should. I will be better soon, I promise. You being here is building up my strength. Stay for me. And look at the books, they can help you…' His eyes closed again, and Olivia sighed. At least he had asked her to stay with him. She could tell Lady Sofia that, and the doctors who had tried to politely hint her away.

She had puzzled for a moment over his mention of the books – what had he meant? There was a huge library in the palace, of course, with books by the thousand, and Olivia often had lessons there. But the message had seemed more important than a reminder to work hard at her lessons.

Then she had remembered that her father had his own small library collection, housed in a tiny room next to his bedchamber. He had explained to Olivia once that the books were his one indulgence, his time away from the duties of ruling the city. The little room was utterly private, and Olivia had not been certain whether she would be able to get inside it without her father.

She had stood hesitating by the door, with her hand on the moulded lock plate, wondering if the magic would let her in. And then the door had swung open. The room felt like the essence of her father, and the books called to her, rich and enticing. Spells whispered out of them, coiling around her lovingly, like Lucian's mane. They wanted to be spoken, they wanted her power for their own.

Olivia had stepped inside the room, and spun around, dizzy with so many possibilities. And then she saw what her father meant for her to do. She had no idea whether he could sense from her magic what she had found in the waters of his city, but he had trusted her with all this power.

So she was going to use it.

She had piled his bed high with delicious volumes,

the dull leather of their bindings gleaming in the candlelight. She spent hours, curled up by his side, trying to find better spells for the rope to climb out of her window, and then discounting that idea entirely – how much better if she could simply fly! But the only flying spell that she could find seemed to require several hundred slaves to be chanting for the entire time that she was afloat. In the end, Olivia compromised, enchanting one of her father's fine linen handkerchiefs – because his were a great deal larger than hers. When the words of the spell were spoken, the linen square would become lighter than air, so light that if she held the corners, and simply jumped out of her bedroom window, she would float down to the water. A little negotiation of the breeze blowing along the canal, and she should be able to land on that useful jetty a little further along.

That was the plan, anyway. Olivia was hoping that she would see Lucian before she jumped. Someone to catch her if it all went wrong would be helpful. She had practised, a little, but climbing to the top of a painted chest filled with spare blankets was hardly the same as jumping out of a window, even if she had felt the handkerchief pull her up before her feet touched the floor. The canal was an awfully long way down. Since their first meeting, she had spent her few spare moments staring out of her bedroom window at the dark water, hoping to see a glimmer of white in the depths, but there had been no sign of the water horse. Olivia thought that the magic of her handkerchief spell floating over the water might call him to help her. She hoped so…

Now she looked thoughtfully at the doll, and twitched her hair a little more, so it lay over the waxen face. Then she placed the palms of her hands against the doll's cool cheeks, and stared into the dark glass eyes, thinking hard. The spell book with the gilded red leather binding had been hard to read, written in faded ink in a spiky, old-fashioned hand, but from some of the phrases Olivia had been sure that it was written by a woman, perhaps even a young girl. She'd had the strangest feeling as she read, a sense that she was not reading at all, but that the girl was standing behind her, and breathing the words into her ear. They were tricksy, deceptive things, those spells, nothing like the formal rituals that her tutors had been drumming into her for years. Their magic was light, and delicate, but full of clever little hooks. Olivia couldn't help wondering if Lady Sofia had her own copy. She had never noticed her father using spells like these, and she wondered where the book had come from.

How to charm another's tongue, so they would speak the words you wanted them to say. How to speak in their own voice yourself. How to walk through a crowded room and not be seen. And how to charm a lifeless image to move and speak like oneself.

It was this spell that Olivia had learned, curled up at the foot of her father's bed with one of the woollen blankets from the painted chest wrapped around her shoulders. It was very rare that one of her ladies-in-waiting should come to her rooms after she had retired for the night, but it had been known to happen. If – and even thinking about it made Olivia squeeze her eyes tight shut to force back her tears – if her father were to relapse again, then someone might come looking for her. She had left orders with the physicians, and she had been very careful to let them see her magic, just a hint of it, in case they thought they didn't need to listen to a little girl.

So if anyone came to find her, they would be greeted by the doll, charmed to yawn and stretch and growl irritably, like a princess woken from her sleep. And a second part of the spell would summon Olivia back to the palace immediately.

The doll was ready. Olivia had on her torn and dirty petticoat again – but now it had been magically darkened to a dull grey, far more suitable for a servant girl. Olivia leaned cautiously out of her window, with the handkerchief clutched tightly against her front. The side of the palace looked a great deal higher than that pretty painted chest in her father's rooms.

'My lady!'

Olivia squeaked, and whirled round, thinking that she had been caught out already, but then she realised that the voice came from below her, in the water.

Lucian was there. That swirl of whiteness she had taken for the wind rippling the water. He rose up, his huge front hooves beating excitedly at the darkness.

'I knew you would come,' he called, and then let out a high, sharp whinny of excitement, echoing back and forth between the old stone walls.

'I'm coming down!' Olivia hissed to him. 'It's a spell – but if it doesn't work you might need to rescue me again.' She opened out the flimsy square of linen, and looked at it doubtfully. Her spells almost always worked, but they didn't usually involve the risk of death. The fine weaving glittered, though, and it fluttered as it caught the breeze blowing off the lagoon. It *would* work, she told herself, as she clutched at the stone frame of the window, and stepped out into nothing.

As she fell, she saw Lucian rearing in the water again, his eyes wild and his mane snaking around his neck in panic. He darted sideways, kicking up a great spray and froth, and then back again, clearly trying to judge where in the water she would land.

'It's working!' she gasped to him. 'Look, I'll land there!'

She whistled the wind, and it flew at her with a delighted rush, sweeping her past the jetty she had intended, until she landed laughing in a little boat that had been left tied up further down the wall.

The water horse plunged up to her, his eyes reddened. 'A spell, you said! You jumped!'

'And then I flew,' Olivia retorted. 'I landed almost where I meant to.' She tucked the handkerchief away in the front of her dress.

'What's that around your middle?' the horse demanded, nudging the bundle Olivia had tied around her waist. She had wanted her hands left free.

'Food, for Jac and the others. I promised. Though I couldn't find very much – my maid thinks there's something wrong with me, I had such a fancy for bread. It seemed the easiest thing to carry. Will you take me to find them again?' She swallowed. 'I want to hear what they have to say about my father now. He collapsed again, worse than before. He's bedridden, and the palace is – it's like an ants' nest. There was one in the courtyard once, and I watched the page boys stir it up with a stick. Everyone's running here and there, only of course they aren't because it's a palace and no one runs, but you can tell that they want to. The only place that's quiet is my

137

father's suite.' Olivia ran her hands over the water horse's velvet nose for comfort, and then wound her fingers in his mane. 'I'm not sure what will happen if he wakes up. When. When he wakes up. He can't be strong again all at once, but I think he'll need to be...'

Lucian snorted and shook his head. 'Then you will have to give him your strength, small one, won't you? Like you did for that spell out in the lagoon.'

He said it so matter-of-factly that Olivia felt he must be right. She would lend her magic to her father, while he needed it. Whatever rumours were flying about the city, if the people saw him performing the spells and rituals as usual, then surely they would believe the duke was well?

And he will be well, eventually, Olivia told herself, as she climbed on to Lucian's warm back. *I would just be propping him up, that's all*. She shuddered a little, as she remembered the other spells in that book, so full of deceit and charm and danger. 'I'm not doing anything like that,' she muttered. 'I'm helping... It's not the same...'

'You came back, then.' The boy was the only one awake, gazing out at them over the huddled piles of children. Olivia still couldn't work out how many of them there were. They all lay draped over each other like kittens, for the warmth.

'I told you I would,' she said indignantly.

The boy only shrugged as though that meant nothing.

'And I brought food, here.' She undid the bundle, and passed it over to him.

'So you did...' he murmured, lifting out a dainty little roll. 'Palace food, this is. You really do work there.' He eyed her cautiously, clearly expecting her to be angry when she heard what he had to say. 'You want the news again, then? What everyone's saying in the markets, about the duke? So you can report back to your princess?'

'Yes.' Olivia dug her nails into her palms, and she felt Lucian shift beneath her, rocking her a little. 'Would you take me to one of these markets? I want to hear all this for myself.'

He looked at her thoughtfully. 'Perhaps. Word is that the Lady Sofia's to be made regent. Because the

139

duke – well, it's like Zuzanna said. He'll not last much longer.'

'He will,' Olivia snarled back, magic flaring around her in a wave of silver. 'Wait and see.'

Jac shrugged. He didn't even look that impressed by the magic, which was unusual. Olivia had learned to keep it under control most of the time, but just occasionally, her temper got the better of her. The maid she'd had before Etta had left in tears, after she had pricked her mistress with a pin altering a dress, and her whole pot of pins had risen up and flown at her in a squealing cloud. Olivia had stopped the pins before they actually hit Maria, but the girl had still taken it amiss. Lady Sofia had been most annoyed – Olivia suspected that Maria had been in her pay. Olivia had chosen Etta herself.

Jac only sniffed at the showy silver flames. 'Want me to duck you in the water, miss? You might singe.' He eyed her interestedly. 'A good master is he, then, that duke? You care a lot more about him than most servants do for their lords and ladies.'

Olivia nodded cautiously. 'I care about the princess.

140

She's not ready to be the duchess yet. But she'd rather die than let Lady Sofia be in charge,' she added viciously, and all the silvery flames went out with a snap.

'Where do you live?' Olivia asked the next night, as she climbed on to Lucian's back, and tucked away the linen handkerchief in the sleeve of the boy's jacket she was wearing. She had found it abandoned in the courtyard of the palace that morning, and hidden it away under the shawl she was carrying, hoping that its owner would not be in too much trouble for losing it. It was old and grubby, and she suspected it belonged to an apprentice to one of the court doctors, or someone like that. It was perfect for her disguise.

Lucian looked round at her, his dark eyes gleaming liquidly in the moonlight.

'I mean, only if you want to tell me,' Olivia added, suddenly uncomfortable. It was the strangest feeling, caring what someone thought of her, whether they trusted her or not. Did he even like her? A princess never spoke to anyone in this odd, uncertain way. Even the girls closest to her in age among the courtiers were always respectful – they would tell her whatever she wanted to hear, she knew it. How could she truly be friends with people who lied to make her happy? Who had to curtsey every time she came near?

If he wanted, Lucian could probably just tip her off his back into the water. Olivia let out a little gasping laugh at the thought.

'What is it?' the white horse asked curiously.

'I don't know how to talk to you tonight,' Olivia said shyly. 'The first time I saw you, I was so surprised, that I didn't really think about it. And then last night I was just excited, because my spell on the handkerchief worked, and I'd saved the food for the children under the bridge. It felt like I was doing something important, bringing them food. I haven't brought any more tonight – I haven't been able to save enough yet for them all to share. I wanted to see you, that's all. I wanted to ride along the canals, and talk. But now I feel shy… You're so *old*. And I think you must be made of magic. I've always been taught that I belong to the city, but you're even more part of Venice than I am.' She ran her hand gently over his mane. 'You shouldn't tell me where you live if it's a secret. I won't mind.' She would, but she would try not to.

Lucian twisted his great head back and nuzzled her gently, scratching her cheek with the prickly whiskers round his velvet mouth. 'I don't have a palace, little one. I sleep by the water, like the children under the bridge. But I sleep mostly in the water, half-in, half-out. Like the city, with its feet always in the sea. I sleep on a flight of stone stairs, half-covered by the tide. I'll show you, if you like.' He looked at her sideways. 'Are you disappointed?'

Olivia smiled shyly at him. 'For a little while I wondered if you had a castle deep down in the sea – like mermaids do, in the stories my old nursemaid told me. With a garden of seaweed trees, and mirrors made of mother of pearl... I know that sounds silly. But I thought perhaps all you water horses lived together.' She had been imagining a stable under the sea.

The water horse shook his head, and his white mane streamed in the wind. 'No, we work together, often, but when we're resting, my people hide ourselves away

143

alone. We aren't lonely exactly, but we're quiet, used to our own company. Maybe we're too much alone – I've looked forward to our meetings, little princess. I'd been dreaming my days away for much too long. But now' – he nudged her again – 'your magic is calling to me, I can feel it dancing over the water. The hairs along my back are lifting. My ears are flickering. I feel awake again.'

He turned into a smaller canal, his strong legs slowing, so that he sank a little lower in the water, and Olivia drew up her feet, half kneeling on his broad back. Stretching out in front of them was a dark channel of water, glimmering here and there in the moonlight.

'Here,' Lucian murmured, stepping on to a flight of stone stairs that led right down into the water. 'Wide steps, you see. Perfect to lie on. And the tree whispers to me with the night wind. I've slept here for years.'

Olivia climbed carefully off his back on to one of the higher steps, some way out of the water. 'And no one ever sees you?' she asked doubtfully. He was so big – she couldn't understand how people could miss him.

Lucian stretched out on the step, his mane and tail trailing down into the water. He didn't look at her.

'Sometimes they do. Children, mostly. They catch a glimpse, from the corner of their eye. But then they look again, and tell themselves I was just the wind, flapping an old boat cover. The light catching on the water.' He nudged her gently. 'Waterweed.'

Olivia smiled for a moment, but it seemed so sad. She twirled a strand of his mane around her fingers. 'But once we did know about you?'

'Yes. But that was long before – when the city wasn't built of stone and gold, like it is today. People were closer to the water, then, in their wooden houses.'

'I don't understand how we can have forgotten,' she murmured. 'My father told me that you were just a story. I suppose if no one saw you, for a while, perhaps we would stop believing... But everyone should see you! Couldn't I show them?'

'What would your grand courtiers say, if you told them about me?' Lucian asked her, and she could tell from his voice that he was laughing.

'That I was mad, I suppose. A silly, hysterical little girl.' Olivia sighed. 'And probably that I'd stop all these strange fancies once I was a little older, and married.'

'Mmmm. You're yawning, child. We should go back.'

Olivia climbed wearily on to his back, wrapping a white lock of his mane around her wrist. She was clumsy from missing out on sleep, and it would be so easy to slide soundlessly down Lucian's side, into the glittering water.

She laid her cheek against his neck, her eyes half-closed, lulled by the gentle splashing as he ploughed through the water. The ripples arrowed away from his broad chest – and met more ripples. She blinked, confused, and looked sideways, trying to understand what she was seeing. Then she sat up, slowly, staring all around.

'You said you lived alone…' she whispered.

'So we do,' Lucian told her, nodding to the pale gold horse swimming by his side. 'But when we call, our brothers and sisters come. I called to them tonight. To tell them I'd found you. I would have told them before…' He snorted to himself, warm air steaming from his nostrils. 'But I was enjoying my secret.'

If she had been looking out of her window, she would

have thought it was some strange tide, Olivia decided. Grey and white and golden, the water horses streamed by like wavelets on the water. Each of them gazed at her, and a few of the most daring nuzzled her hand, or stroked their coiling tails around her damp petticoat.

'So many...'

'All of us,' Lucian agreed. 'All of us are yours now, princess. If you need us, we will be here.'

Chapter Eight

'COME ON!'

Olivia looked back anxiously at Lucian, who was watching her from the canal. It was late evening, and not fully dark, much earlier than she had been out with him before. She had retired to bed early, telling her ladies-in-waiting that she had a headache. So many more people were around, and she was nervous.

'Go. You'll be safe with them,' he murmured, sinking down so that only his eyes and ears showed above the water.

'Come on.' The little girl smiled up at Olivia. She

was the youngest, Olivia decided – Zuzanna, the one who would have drowned if Lucian hadn't rescued her. Zuzanna tugged at her hand again. 'Come and see.'

Olivia let the little girl lead her after Jac, who was already disappearing between the stalls. 'Is the market open every night?' she asked curiously.

Zuzanna nodded. 'It's closing now, though. The stallholders stay for people on their way home from work.'

Jac darted out between two awnings, the front of his jacket bulging with bruised and blackened fruit. 'It's a good time to come. They're giving away the stuff they can't sell tomorrow. Or getting as much as they can for it. That's why I bring her. Zuzanna, cry, can't you? Look hungrier.'

Zuzanna crumpled up her face obediently, and Jac nodded. 'Good.'

'Why does she have to cry?' Olivia asked, confused.

'Because then people will feel sorry for her, and give us food!' Jac rolled his eyes. 'You don't know anything, living in that palace. You don't know you're born.'

'Poor little dear.' An old lady leaned over from behind

her stall, and pressed a loaf of bread into Olivia's arms. 'Take your little sister home, girl, feed her that.'

'Many thanks, gracious lady,' Jac nodded to her, and Olivia smiled shyly, and bobbed her head too.

'She should be sleeping, a little one like that. Where are your parents?' the old lady grumbled, and Jac twisted his face into a miserable grimace. 'Our mother is dead, and our father is away with the fleet, gracious lady. The rent's due – we can't afford food as well…'

The old lady sighed. 'I know. Here, take another loaf. I must have given away more than I've sold, today. No one has any money. Did you hear a tax collector was stabbed, earlier this week? I'm not surprised, greedy bloodsuckers that they are.'

Olivia felt her eyes grow round. She wondered if anyone had told her father that. And then she remembered, like swallowing a lump of stone. He was still unconscious, waxen pale in that great golden bed, and every day she told encouraging lies about how well he was recovering.

Did her father have his own spies, out in the city? She supposed he must. But now most of the actual business of the court was being done by the Council of Ten, which meant her aunt. Olivia didn't think that Lady Sofia would approve of lowering taxes, or giving out food to starving families.

At the next stall, two men were discussing the high prices for vegetables, and grumbling that they were worse every day. Not even Zuzanna's most pathetic face got them anything here, and they trailed on. For Olivia, it grew easier and easier to look tired and broken and hungry as they made their way round the market. Her city was grand and beautiful, full of gilded statues, and beautiful dresses. It wasn't a place where children had to beg for food from people who were almost as desperate as they were.

When she had set out to explore the city, that first night, she had thought all this talk of riots would be nothing – just a mistake, just a few old angry women. Whatever it was, she was going to have an adventure, and then she'd go back to the palace, and find some way to make it right.

But there *wasn't* a way. Even if she gave all these hungry people food, they'd still be hungry the next day, and the next. She felt as though the ground was shaking under her feet.

'Olivia…'

Mmmm…? Olivia flicked over a page, and then she jumped, her eyes widening. He had spoken aloud!

'You're awake…' she whispered delightedly, leaning closer to her father.

He smiled at her. 'I had the strangest dreams, sweetling.' He patted at the sleeves of his nightgown. 'So real. I almost feel this should be wet – there were the most amazing creatures, in the water…' He shook his head, and Olivia could see him casting away the water horses as a pretty dream, a fancy from his fevered brain.

'It was real,' she whispered, just as the door banged open, and one of the duke's doctors came hurrying in. 'It was all real. Oh, I wish I could talk to you, but I still don't think you'd believe me…'

When the doctors had left, going back to their laboratories to brew more tonics, and elixirs, more magic cures that wouldn't work, Olivia's father beckoned her closer. 'How long has it been?' he breathed, even the faintest whisper an effort.

'Days,' Olivia admitted reluctantly. 'Almost a week. You collapsed in the night, a few days after the Wedding of the Sea.'

'Her father chuckled hoarsely. 'Is Sofia...enjoying herself?'

Olivia glared at him. She didn't think it was very funny. 'Far too much. She has her own people, you know, all through the court.'

'I know. Will you help me, Olivia? I can't be seen like this – there will be ceremonies, rituals to perform. I can't even stand, yet. I may need you...'

'We'll do it together,' Olivia promised him. She could see that it hurt him to have to ask. 'You know my aunt wants Zuan to inherit, not me,' she added suddenly.

'That will never happen,' her father told her, and his voice was stronger this time. 'Sofia has always been ambitious – too ambitious. She's my sister, and I love her, even with her manipulative ways. But you are the heir. Sofia has always wanted you to marry Zuan, but I have my doubts about the match, the boy seems not to

153

have inherited his mother's skill. There may be a cruel streak, even... Sofia will see that, one day – she wants the best for our city, as I do.'

Olivia stared at him, his head resting against the embroidered pillows, his hands gesturing weakly. He sounded so sure – but she *knew* that Lady Sofia had been putting spells on her for years. Her aunt wanted the best for Zuan, and Mia. Not the city. Olivia opened her mouth, about to tell him – but he looked so sick. His skin was stretched waxy yellow over his bones, and his eyes were deeply sunken. Every breath seemed to be an effort. She wasn't sure her father was strong enough to hear the truth.

Olivia sat curled up with her back against the stonework of the bridge. Lucian lay next to her. It was one of the few times she had seen him completely out of the canal – although he still had one foreleg dangling over the lip of the stones, the hoof trailing in the water. Only now could she see just how huge he was.

'Is the water rising?' she asked him, peering out of their cave-like shelter under the bridge. The faint pearly glow of his coat lit up the stonework and shone on the water – but it only made the dark seem darker.

'Yes.' He shook his mane fiercely. 'I wanted to keep you here until the storm was over, princess. But I need to be in the water. Without us holding it back, the storm surge will be too great. The city's defences won't hold.'

'I should go back anyway,' Olivia sighed, gazing out reluctantly at the grey sheets of rain. She couldn't even see the drops, the fall was so heavy. 'Father is awake.'

Lucian shoved her gently with his shoulder. 'I heard him.'

Olivia sat up to look at him better. 'You did? How?'

'I can sense your magic running through the water. How do you think I know to be there when you want to go jumping out of windows?'

Olivia smiled to herself. Lucian still distrusted her floating spell, even now that he had seen her work it several times. But then, she didn't trust it entirely either – she stood hesitating on the window ledge each night. She still couldn't always say exactly where she would land, but the spell worked well enough for getting down. On that first night she had tried to use it to carry her back up. It should have worked, she was sure, but the spell had faltered, and only lifted her a little off her feet. Lucian had to lift her, rather smugly calling a great wave to cast them both up so she could tumble through the window. After that she had left another rope, spelled to look like the stones of the wall.

'Now your magic is mixed with another – older, and more fixed. Your father's, I guessed.'

'Fixed?' Olivia frowned at him.

The great horse shrugged, flicking his forelock out of his eyes. 'Very strong, but set in his ways. Everything always the same. Like those ceremonies you keep on having. Trumpets and boats and flowers.'

Olivia nodded slowly. If she hadn't met a water horse, she suspected her own magic would have gone the same way.

'That's how we've always done things...' she murmured, leaning down against his shoulder again, and wrapping her arm around his neck. 'The rituals hold back the waters, or do other things to keep the city going. There's another one in two days' time. Father has told the council that of course he can do it… He had to – after he'd not been in public for all those days, he couldn't let them see how exhausted he is still. He held an audience for the Talish ambassador this morning, just to show that he could.'

'So actually it will be you working the spells.' Lucian blew gently over her hair. 'Are you strong enough?'

'I think so.' But her voice was very small. 'After the Wedding of the Sea – I loved it, while we were making the spell, but then I was so tired. All of me was…like after you cry for a long time, and you ache, inside and out.'

'Horses don't cry… Time to go back, my lady, I need to be in the water. I'll watch for you tomorrow. Remember all of us in the water.' He nosed at her again. 'I may sneer a little at your ceremonies, dear one, but there is a power to them. If we could mix your father's way and mine, the floods might settle.'

Wet and bedraggled, Olivia caught at the stones of the window with slippery fingers, and then hauled herself back in. She was so cold! Every other time she had been out, Lucian had somehow managed to keep her warm. He never seemed to get properly wet, even when he'd been underwater. But tonight the rain had been so heavy that even he had looked uncomfortable as he swam away. She had watched him dive deep down into the canal, throwing back a swirl of muddy silt.

She tumbled on to the floor of her bedroom, and sighed wearily. It was all the nights spent exploring her city, first of all taking food to the children under the bridge, and then hiding with Lucian under more bridges and behind boats. They had listened to gossip from old ladies on their verandas, and courting couples leaning over parapets. All the spying hadn't told Olivia a great deal more than the children had, but it had filled her with a sense of determination, and love. Venice felt more like her city than it ever had before. It was up to her to make things right – once her father was stronger again, she would find some way to explain to him what she had seen, and that the city would have to change. She would have to. Her father must already *know*, she had realised slowly, sadly. He must understand that people were hungry, and angry, even if he didn't see quite how bad things were. Had it always been that way? Olivia couldn't understand why he hadn't done anything about it. But then, she wouldn't have cared either, if she hadn't been shocked out of her happy dream-life by a resentful maid at a party, and a hungry old woman.

Wrapping her arms around herself, she leaned her head against the wall. She would get up in a moment. She needed to clean herself up…

'My lady, where have you *been*?'

Olivia sat up so fast she nearly fell over. Etta was standing beside her, looking horrified.

'Oh… I fell asleep at the window, Etta.' She tried to stand up, but her feet were still asleep, clumsy with pins and needles.

'You didn't, you weren't here! I went looking everywhere for you, and now I find you by the window. You climbed back in, didn't you? You weren't here!'

'Well, why were *you* here?' Olivia demanded, as Etta pulled her upright, and fussed around her, leading her to a cushioned chair.

'I crept back in to fetch your lilac gloves. You stained

them, and I forgot to take them to Ma to clean.'

Olivia glanced at the curtained bed. The curtains were a little open, and she could see the doll, sleeping sweetly in her place.

'How did you know that wasn't me?' she asked, too curious to be angry.

Etta stopped, and looked. 'I don't know...' She sounded honestly puzzled. 'I suppose – you don't sleep like that, my lady.'

'I hope you're not telling me that I snore,' Olivia said coldly.

'Certainly not! No... It's not that. She looks so peaceful. You dream, my lady. You toss about. And even when you're sleeping deep, you don't look like that.' Etta nodded. 'Yes. That's your old doll, my lady. The one from the top of your dressing table. You've just changed her a bit.'

'Oh.'

'I won't tell, my lady. And it's a very good likeness, for someone who's never seen you asleep.'

'Well, I suppose I haven't ever seen me asleep either. You could probably make ever such a lot of money telling my aunt,' Olivia pointed out, but Etta shuddered.

'Not her, my lady! I never trusted her, even before I saw her putting spells on you. She makes my hair itch.'

'*What?*'

'Mmm. It lifts up a little, and it itches.' Etta eyed her mistress nervously, and then added, in a gabbled whisper. 'Her son, too. The only one of them I like is that little girl Mia.'

'Me too,' Olivia sighed. 'You know I'm supposed to marry him, don't you?'

Etta was silent. 'My lady, were you slipping out to meet…a boy?'

'Of course not!' Olivia stared at her.

'Because if you were, I'd say you should run away with him now. Even if he's ugly and pox-scarred and lazy. You don't ever want to end up married to that Lord Zuan. I mean it, my lady. Not even for a city.'

'I know.' Olivia found that her voice had gone very small. 'I'm doing my best, Etta. It wasn't a boy I met, though. It was a horse. There are horses who live in the water, did you know that?'

Etta was looking at her sceptically, and Olivia smiled. 'You think I've been dreaming, don't you?'

'It wouldn't surprise me if there was all sorts of things out there, my lady. You'd better take that ragged thing off so I can wash and dry it. I can't take that to the laundry, can I?'

CHAPTER NINE

EVEN WITH THE WATER horses working to coax back the tide, the waters kept rising. Olivia drifted off to sleep again listening to the rain hammering against her shutters, and the shouts of the men out piling up bags of sand around the doorways. The city was rousing in panic as the floods began to seep into the houses at the water's edge. In her dreams, she saw their people turning towards the palace, eyes filled with fear. Why was the duke letting this happen?

When Etta woke her the next morning, they went together to the front of the palace to see the water lapping just below the windows, and people struggling across the square knee-deep. Their faces were pale and frightened, and many of them were carrying bags and precious belongings. One old woman had a canary in a cage. They were leaving their houses, going to stay with family and friends who lived higher up. But nowhere in Venice was safe from the waters, Olivia thought, biting her lip. She could smell the fear, rising out of the city. Panic, and anger… They couldn't let it go on.

'It hasn't been this bad in years,' Etta murmured.

'My lady!' A page boy came running, his stockings already soaked. 'The duke requests your presence. At once.'

Olivia followed him to the terrace along the first floor, where her father stood, leaning heavily on the marble balustrade beneath the pointed arches. He was quite alone, wrapped in a dark gown. No one glancing up as they cursed their way across the flooded square would take him for the duke. He looked like some weary courtier, wondering if the water had already got in his front door.

'Wait there for me, Etta,' Olivia murmured, hurrying

towards him. 'Father, should you be out here? It's cold.'

He wrapped one arm around her, and she felt how thin it was under the heavy velvet sleeve. 'I don't think cold has much to do with my weakness, dearest. Olivia, we have to do something about this. Tomorrow we bless the fountains, and you know that will be hard for me.' His arm tightened around her. 'If I'm to manage those spells, I must save my strength. I can't do anything to send the waters back. I hate to ask this of you, when you're still so young. I know I've already called on your magic enough, just to be here.'

Olivia took a breath, almost ready to tell him about the water horses, and the chance they had to use the old magic of the water to work with the tides, instead of always binding back the power of the water the way they did. But she couldn't. Her father was so protective, because he still thought of her as a little girl. How could she confess to him that she had been exploring the city by night, and consorting with a gang of beggar children, and a wild water horse? There would be an uproar. And her father would consult his dear sister, who had raised Olivia from a baby – together with a palaceful of servants. He would ask her aunt what to do, and Lady Sofia would tell him that Zuan's steadying influence would be just what Olivia needed. Nobly-born girls were expected to marry young, and they could be promised to their future husbands from birth. Once they were formally betrothed, she would never be able to get out of it.

Olivia hadn't told her father that she refused the marriage yet. Lady Sofia had been whispering to him about it for years. Her father had told her that he wasn't sure about Zuan, so she had hope, but he still loved and trusted Lady Sofia, his closest companion since his wife had died. Olivia couldn't tell him all at once that she hated Zuan, and her aunt, and feared them both. Not now, when the duke was so weak and ill.

So all she said was, 'I can work the spell. What do I have to do?'

'Come.' Her father led her along the terrace, and the harassed, damp page boy hurried ahead of them, shooing people away, until they came to the great entrance that led down towards the Grand Canal.

'You need to stand in the water. Is this a dress that

matters?' the duke asked, looking at Olivia's rose pink silk thoughtfully. 'Perhaps you could lift it up?'

Olivia nodded, and kicked off the matching pink slippers, as she looked at the grey, sulky water. It seemed to be creeping towards her even now, lapping hungrily at the marble steps. She didn't want to put her feet in it. It seemed so different from the sparkling, foaming stuff that Lucian galloped through, with her riding high on his back.

'Your silk stockings, my lady,' Etta hissed, darting forward, and crouching down to help her pull them off. 'Even my ma couldn't bring them clean after soaking in that.'

Olivia stood barefoot, her rosy dress gathered up over her arms, and stretched out her toes towards the water. It sucked at her greedily, and she shuddered as she stepped down into the swirling greyness.

'Listen,' her father murmured, and all at once she seemed to hear the spell in her mind, the right way to push and scoop and banish the water, back to the sea and the ships, back to where it belonged.

But there was so much, and it was so heavy... And

167

she couldn't help feeling that this was wrong, that it wasn't the way. If only she could gallop through the water like the horses, leading it with her, instead of pushing it away...

Olivia stared out into the lagoon, fighting with the dull expanse of water, and feeling it fight back. She could sense her father's magic, weary and anxious, pushing behind her, and she wanted to turn and scream at him to stop, to let her do it alone, that if she hadn't the strength, then certainly neither had he.

Then the little white wave crests settled and reformed, and she saw what she had been looking at, out in the lagoon just beyond the line of moored boats; Lucian, and a crowd of other white horses, watching her. She could almost hear them whinnying above the wind. She ached to dive deeper into the water, to swim out with them, and play.

'Help me...' she called, sending her voice out into the tearing gusts, and all at once the weight of the water lessened as they pawed at the waves, calling the flood back to the sea.

'Gold is your colour, my lady,' Etta cooed, as she fussed with Olivia's laces, and smoothed the glittering brocade. 'So beautiful.'

'I shall look like part of the gondola,' Olivia muttered, peering into the mirror. 'That's all gold too. And all I have to do is sit still, everyone will just think I'm a statue.'

'You're pale enough to be marble.' Etta tutted, looking over her shoulder. Then she ducked her head anxiously.

Olivia wondered if Etta had heard the story about the pins. She probably had. 'It's all right,' she said wearily. 'You're only telling the truth. You know I hardly slept last night.' She rubbed fiercely at her cheeks. 'Ow... Is that better?'

'A little, my lady,' Etta said doubtfully. 'I could always fetch a rabbit's foot, and a little carmine?'

'No. I'm sure half the court would be able to tell,' Olivia sighed. 'I'll just pinch my cheeks when no one's looking. We had better go, I can hear them fussing outside.'

The blessing of the fountains called for the duke and

his daughter – and most of the court – to be rowed around the city, along the canals, stopping at the old stone water fountains. The duke would take a sip from each, and work a spell to preserve the sweetness of the water for another year. On good years, the spells were hardly worn at all, but the flooding had turned many of the old wells brackish. The people of the city were out in their thousands, waiting eagerly for the duke to bring their water back, pure and sweet.

The day wore on, and Olivia smiled regally, and waved, and watched her father grow paler and paler as each spell drew out a little more of his strength. She poured her magic after him as much as she could, but the poisoned water drained them both. Lucian was in the water close by – she suspected, from the silvery bubbles rising on either side, that he was gliding along underneath the gondola – but his magic was with the water of the canal, not the deep, sweet water in the marshy ground under the city. His presence strengthened her a little, but that was all.

She was so tired, as the afternoon shadows grew longer, that she forgot where they were. Had she been

170

wider awake, she would have seen the beaming fishes, leaping among the carved stone flourishes of the bridge. But as it was, she gazed fixedly ahead, her teeth showing in a weary grimace of a smile, as they glided into the cool shadows under the bridge.

Then something tugged at her – a memory, and a sense of danger – and she turned her head a little, to see the children staring.

They were there, under the bridge, just as they had been before. Little Zuzanna was clapping her hands to see the pretty boats go past, but the others drew her back deeper into the shadows. They were not supposed to be this close to the royal party – some guard had lapsed, and forgotten to chase the pack of beggars away. Olivia smiled, and raised her hand to wave – and then she remembered that she was a princess, not a serving girl; the girl they knew was Livi. Except that Livi looked just like Olivia, even in gold brocade, with pearls woven in her hair. Zuzanna was waving at her now and smiling, but the older ones looked shocked, and Jac was clearly angry. Furious. She could see him cursing as the boat glided on regardless, leaving the bridge and the children behind.

Olivia wanted to call back, to explain, but she couldn't. Instead she stared silently ahead, her smile still in place.

Then a muffled exclamation from the oarsman behind made her turn and gasp. Behind them, the waters were surging up in a great whirlpool, lashing and angry, and clearly the work of a magician. The other boats in their little fleet were tossed across the water, several of them overturned, their passengers screaming in the water. Her cousin Zuan was clinging to an oar, struggling to stay above the surface. He fought his way up on to the side of a boat, and Olivia watched him turn to stare at the little gang of children by the bridge. His eyes were murderous.

Her father stood up, and raised his hand, but staggered as the first wash hit the gondola, sending it slewing sideways. Olivia could feel him, sending all his strength to those in the water, holding them up. She wanted to scream at him to stop, to save himself instead.

She hit the wooden side of the boat and gasped, all thoughts of counterspells driven from her mind. Her hand trailed in the water, and then she felt them, surging towards her. Lucian erupted from the depths of the canal, and she saw the full power of his water magic for the first time. He reared up with an eerie shriek, and then struck the surface with his glistening hooves. The water around the gondola stilled at once, and Olivia saw the other water horses nudging the people in the water back towards their boats, even pushing them back aboard. The puzzled courtiers stared around, obviously not sure how they had been saved. Olivia thought she saw one or two people blink, and lean out, and stare, as if they had caught a glimpse of the white and golden creatures darting about amongst the wreckage.

Then the water horses plunged away, galloping at full pelt around the rocking boats, and on, on down the canal, taking the storm surge with them before it could attack anyone else.

Olivia looked back at the bridge, but it was empty – the children were gone.

CHAPTER TEN

'CAN YOU SEE THEM?' Olivia murmured, peering forward between Lucian's flickering ears, into the darkness of the night. The water was eerily calm, with fragments of wood from broken boats scattered across it still. The Bridge of the Smiling Fishes stood quiet, with no children gathered sleeping underneath.

'No. They've moved on.' Lucian nosed thoughtfully at something half-floating in the water – a thin embroidered scarf, dark and sodden now. Olivia blinked at it, trying to remember if she had seen it on one of the girls from the court.

'This was all my fault,' she whispered. 'I made Jac angry. I made him trust me, and then I lied to him.'

'This wasn't you...' Lucian let out a long, whistling breath. 'Your family, though, perhaps. The dukes have grown stronger, and stronger, and the people's magic has dwindled away. Your family have cared for the city's finances, and the warships, and the grand buildings. But they've twisted the magic, and set it into narrow ways... And the city doesn't take care of its small ones any more.'

'I will,' Olivia promised him quietly. 'If you'll help me.' She reached down and pulled out the dripping scarf, winding it around her hands. 'Where did Jac's magic come from, Lucian? He is a magician, even though he laughed at me when I said so. Look at what he can do!' She shivered.

Lucian snorted. 'Of course he is. And his magic came from the same place as yours. The city – the sea – the waters all around you. He's very strong, that one. Magic doesn't only belong to the grand people, little princess.' But he looked round at her fondly as he said it.

'It feels like everything I've been taught is wrong,'

175

Olivia murmured sadly. 'Even Father said that the magic was in our blood. That it was our family who made Venice what it is.'

'Proud and powerful, yes. And cold.' Lucian turned his head slowly from side to side. 'Jac is dangerous as well as strong. All that water magic, but he doesn't think about it the way you do. He doesn't have the same rules. Where *are* those children?'

'I should think they're hiding,' Olivia suggested. 'Enough people saw Jac standing there at the time. No one at the palace really knows what happened. Most of the courtiers are saying it was some sort of freak storm. Maybe even a whirlwind, I heard one of the council telling Father. Really, a whirlwind? When have we ever had one of those? But I know my aunt and Zuan saw Jac.' She sighed. 'I'm almost sure that everyone will blame it on Father somehow, though. Something wrong with the magic again. They'll say he let it happen, because he's weak, and ill. The whispers – they aren't just whispers any more.' She laid her hand on the smooth hair of Lucian's neck, feeling the muscles move under her fingers. 'I'm scared for Jac,' she murmured. 'I know what he did was awful, but if my aunt sends the palace guards or the city force after him and they catch him they'll do worse things. They won't care that I made him angry. Even Father...' Olivia trailed off, and then forced herself to say the words. 'Even Father would be glad to have someone else to blame...' she added, in a halting voice.

'We'll keep looking.' Lucian swished his tail from side to side, and Olivia flinched as it snapped through the night air like a whip. 'I can feel them, somewhere...' he murmured, as he swam on away from the bridge. 'Not that far.' He pawed at the water with frustration. 'Close, but not close. Somehow removed... And frightened.'

'Oh, we have to find them! Not just to keep them safe – they could help, don't you think? We already know that Jac's water magic is stronger than anything most of our court could do. Imagine if all the others are like that too! They could help hold back the floods.' She frowned. 'I don't understand why they haven't done it already. Jac said the floods stole away their sleeping places, but if he can control the water like that, why didn't he just make the floods go down?'

'He didn't know he could, until he got angry. He probably didn't intend to overturn those boats at all.' Lucian sighed wearily. 'It's no good, Olivia. I can't find them, and it's late. You need to get back to the palace.'

Olivia smoothed his flattened ears. 'Thank you.'

'What for?' The water horse turned to look at her in surprise.

'Everything. You stopped the gondola capsizing this afternoon, but not just that – for rescuing me the very first time. For showing me your water magic. And for telling me things, most of all that. I hate to think about the way I was, before I knew you, and I listened to Etta. I changed a little at New Year, after I broke my aunt's spells, but not all that much. I was still so... selfish. I never thought about things properly. Not till I talked to you.

'Lucian, are there other creatures we've forgotten about, living in the water?' she added suddenly. Why had she never asked him before?

He snorted. 'Forgotten, or never knew about at all?

Of course. There are things in the deep waters that even I don't understand.'

'Oh… I've dreamed about them sometimes, I think.'

'Dreams can be dark magic, even darker than the water.' Lucian nudged his velvet nose against her cheek, and turned for home. 'Be very careful. And now I must take you back, before you're missed. Look, the sky's growing lighter already.'

'Ha.' Olivia laughed wearily. 'Why did you have to tell me that it was so late? Now I can't stop yawning. Etta will complain about my bad colour again.'

'Back home soon,' the horse murmured softly, and the rocking motion as he swam sent her drowsing against his great neck, with his mane wrapped round holding her tight.

There was a grey half-light over the water as he stopped beneath her window, and woke her with gentle nibbling tugs at her damp hair. 'Sshh. The city's waking, child. Back to your bed, before you're found. I'll keep looking for the children under the bridge.'

Olivia nodded, too dazed with sleep to be scared as the water surged up, and the great horse stilled outside the window, waiting for her to catch the rope, and haul herself safely home.

But the scent of her room was wrong, the feel. There was other magic, eager and clutching, and there was a face at her window, with a rope of pearls crowning dark and shining hair – a face pale with triumphant anger.

Olivia screamed. 'Lucian, go! Don't let them catch you! Go!'

She was hanging on to the stonework around the window, scrabbling for the handkerchief to lift her safe away, but there were arms around her waist, and the smell of her aunt's oil of roses, and she knew she was caught.

The white horse was falling back – she watched his wave collapse down, and heard his anguished scream, as he disappeared under the water. But then he resurfaced, gazing up at her and frantically clawing at the stones of the wall with his hooves.

'Go, please!' she called, making one last effort to fight against Lady Sofia.

'I will come back for you!' The whinnying voice rang

in her ears, as she was dragged into the room.

'Who were you talking to? Where have you been?' her aunt screamed.

Olivia glanced at the bed. She was so exhausted, but her heart was hammering. The doll spell hadn't worked – what had gone wrong? How had they caught her?

The toy lay scattered across the bedspread in pieces, and Olivia felt suddenly sick. The waxen arms were still so flesh-like, with the last traces of the broken spell clinging on. She had loved that doll so much – it was a present from her father.

'Let me go, at once,' she said, so coldly that her aunt did as she was told for a moment. But then she seized Olivia's arm again.

'Are there more of them?' Lady Sofia demanded. 'Did you let one of them slip?' she added, turning to the shadows by the door. Olivia gasped. She had not seen Zuan standing there, still in the ruined clothes he had worn that afternoon, his hair flattened and streaked across his face.

'No. We got all of them. I tracked them most carefully. I promise you, Mother.'

'Who?' Olivia glanced between them. The water horses? Could her aunt and her cousin see them after all?

'Then who else was she with? Tell me!' Lady Sofia snarled, still ignoring her, just jerking her back as she tried to pull away. 'The boy who cast the spell knew her, it was clear. What was going on, you stupid girl? They attacked you! Why on earth would you help them escape!'

Then Olivia realised. They didn't mean the horses at all. 'Oh!' She pressed her hand against her mouth, fighting another wave of sickness. 'Jac! You caught Jac!'

'She does know him!' Zuan stepped forward angrily. 'Is this some sort of plot against your father?'

Olivia laughed angrily. The anger was good. It surged through her, and she stood up straighter, refusing to let Lady Sofia see how much the grip on her arm burned. 'The only ones plotting against my father are the two of you,' she snapped. 'Jac is a street child, that's all. The spell was a mistake. He was angry because I lied to him – I went out in disguise, Aunt. To find out what was happening in the city. There were so many frightening rumours, after Father collapsed. I had to see what was really happening! I talked to the children, that's all. They did nothing wrong!'

'Nothing!' Lady Sofia snarled furiously. 'Your cousin nearly drowned, you stupid, reckless girl. And who was out there just now, if it wasn't another of that gang?'

Olivia swallowed. She wanted to tell her father about the water horses, not her aunt. She could just imagine what Lady Sofia and Zuan would do, if they understood the secrets of the water. They'd find some way to chain Lucian and the others, and they'd use them, she knew it. 'Lucia. A servant girl, rowing her way to work,' she said disgustedly. 'She was kind enough to take a longer way, and bring me home. And then you terrified her.'

Lady Sofia didn't know whether to believe her or not. Olivia could see the uncertainty flickering in the honey-coloured eyes. She raised her free hand to her chest, covering the pendant that was hidden under her dark cloak, and pressing it tightly into her skin. *Wrap me up, and hide me away from her… Don't let her see what I've been doing…*

'What have you done with those children?' she demanded aloud.

'Imprisoned them, of course.' Lady Sofia nodded at the window, and Olivia looked out at the opposite wall in horror. Those little children – even Zuzanna, the baby – shut up in the dank cells on the other side of the water.

'Release them at once! They had nothing to do with me disappearing! I shall go and tell my father to let them go!'

'You will stay in your room. And I shall have this window locked and barred,' Lady Sofia growled. 'Sly little thing. Deceitful. *I* shall tell your father, I shall tell him just what you have been doing.' She smiled, and her mouth curved perfectly, her teeth glittered white. But her eyes were hard. 'Or I would, if he were able to hear me.'

'Father!' Olivia gasped.

'Yes, he collapsed again while you were out on your little jaunt. Wouldn't it be a pity if the last he knew was that you had disappeared, kidnapped by a gang of murderous ruffians?'

Olivia plunged towards the door, but Zuan seized her, laughing, and twisting her arm cruelly behind her back. 'You're staying *here*.'

CHAPTER ELEVEN

OLIVIA SAT CURLED IN THE middle of her bed, still with the broken pieces of the doll around her. Lady Sofia and Zuan between them had worked a spell across her window, a lattice of cruel stinging wires that try as she might, she could not undo. Her bedroom door was locked, and all she could do was watch the dawn light shimmer through the spell.

I'm sorry, Father... Can you hear me, this far away? I don't think my aunt Sofia cares any more, if people see what she's trying to do. I think she's gone beyond that now. But I'm safe! Whatever she told you, it wasn't true! I'm safe, and

I think I've found a way to help. Please believe me…

If only she could think harder, and send the message to him more strongly!

Then she was jolted out of her concentration. Something had twitched. It was moving, over on the other side of the room, by the door into her wardrobe. Olivia watched in disgust as something brownish crawled across the floor. A rat! She had seen them before, occasionally, but always at a safe distance, scuttling away along the canal banks. She had never been within touching distance of one, biting distance. She drew her feet closer in, and watched it inch closer. Was it sick? It was moving very slowly.

The rat mewed, and Olivia gasped. Not a rat at all – a kitten!

'Coco!' She sprang off the bed, scurrying to reach him, and scoop up the tiny huddle of dusty fur. 'What did they do to you?' she whispered.

He mewed again, and struggled in her hands, clawing at her faintly. His eyes opened, round and blue, but they were unfocused, the pupils huge.

Olivia cupped her hands around him, and began to

mutter a spell for healing – something so simple it should have taken seconds. But she ached all over, exhausted by the water spells, and then the night of searching, and the tearing at the window spell that shut her in. All that happened was that Coco's battered whiskers straightened out and shimmered, and a faint scent of chocolate filled the room. And the kitten would not stop struggling.

'I'm trying to make you better!' Olivia protested as he stabbed her with one sharp and tiny claw. 'No, don't!'

He had leapt out of her hands, a desperate jump that sent him crumpling to the floor. But he struggled up, and began crawling determinedly away before she could catch him. And then he looked back at her, almost angrily, and she realised what was happening. He was trying to get her to follow him. Olivia hurried across the room, her heart thumping painfully against her ribs.

'Etta!' She half-screamed it. Her maid had fallen in the doorway of the wardrobe, with her hands still up against her face. She had been trying to stop someone hitting her.

'Zuan,' Olivia whispered. 'He did this. Oh, Etta,

you were even more right about him than I knew.'

Coco huddled himself under Etta's chin, and his dazed blue eyes slid closed again. Olivia stared at them both, horrified. One side of Etta's face was swollen and bruised, and there was dried blood at the corner of her mouth.

'How could they be so cruel?' Olivia murmured, tenderly stroking Etta's hair. 'Couldn't they just have sent you on an errand? Or told the guards to take you away? They didn't have to hurt you.'

'I fought back,' Etta whispered hoarsely, as Olivia's magic silvered faintly over the purple of the bruise. 'I made him angry.'

'I hate him, Etta. I will hurt him back,' Olivia whispered viciously, and the fury lifted her magic and strengthened it, so that it surged across Etta's damaged face, making her squeak.

'I didn't mean to do that!'

'You don't know your own strength,' Etta muttered faintly. 'My lady, the kitten, I've just remembered!' She struggled, trying to sit up. 'That beast Lord Zuan, he kicked him. Where is he?'

189

'Here, Etta, he's snuggling up to you, but he's hurt. You hold him, look. He wouldn't keep still for me, I hadn't seen you hidden away in here, and he made me follow him.'

'I crawled away from them,' Etta admitted. 'I was frightened.'

'Good. If you hadn't, I don't know what they would have done. Zuan is cruel enough to have killed you, I know he is. And he thinks he can get away with anything. Oh, Etta, Coco's legs...'

'Can't you mend him?' Etta begged, as together they looked down at the broken little creature. 'Please, my lady?'

Olivia set her hands around her maid's, and closed her eyes, dragging up everything she could. At the back of her mind she knew that it was not sensible, that the kitten was too badly injured, perhaps even dying. It wouldn't work. She should save her strength – there were so many other things she needed to do. She should break out of her room, and mend her father, and hold back the floodwater, and rescue her friends.

But Etta had stood up to Lady Sofia, and Zuan.

Etta had fought, even though she had nothing to fight with. Etta had trusted her.

She would try to save Etta's precious kitten, even if she knew that it was hopeless. Etta would see her try. She gasped as the magic burned across the skin of her fingers, and then it was gone.

'My lady!' Etta cried sharply, and Olivia opened her eyes slowly, not wanting to see that same broken ball of fur. Except it wasn't there.

'What happened?' She gaped at Etta's empty hands.

'I don't know! There was a burning, and then something flashed, and my eyes went odd, the way they do if you look at the sun...'

'And now he's gone,' Olivia finished, in a small, miserable voice. 'Etta, I'm so sorry, I don't know what I did.'

She expected Etta to be angry – but no, of course she wouldn't be, not out loud. She would say it didn't matter, and she would pretend, but she would still be devastated deep down. Olivia glanced at Etta's hands – hands were harder to control than faces. But Etta's hands hung loosely in her lap, and as she saw Olivia looking, she stretched one hand out, very tentatively, and patted her cheek. 'You tried for me…'

Then Olivia saw her mouth curl, and her eyes lightened. The colour flushed across her cheeks, staining the bruises suddenly darker. 'My lady, look!' She took her hand from Olivia's cheek and pointed behind her, to the bed.

And when Olivia turned, there was a very large, very grown-up chocolate-brown cat sitting grandly between the curtains, and staring down at them with clear blue eyes.

Etta lay sleeping next to her, with Coco tucked under her arm. Olivia didn't think he was asleep, or not completely, anyway. His tail twitched, every so often. Etta was warm. It was odd, how different it felt, sleeping with someone next to her. Her room was never cold, of course. She would have made a terrible fuss if it had been. But the warmth of a person was different. She almost envied the children under the bridge, sleeping curled together every night. Etta slept the way the doll had, too, peaceful and sweet. Even if she had been beaten, and her mistress was imprisoned, and there was a plot…

Olivia drowsed, and dreamed…

You're there! At last…

Olivia sat up, and felt the roughness of the embroidered doublet against her cheek again. Her father was sitting on the edge of her bed, looking down at her curled against his chest, and smiling; a taller, younger, happier father. The way she remembered him from when she was little, from when he had told her the story of the water horses.

Olivia, you must not let Sofia force you to marry that boy.

'Father! Are you better? Are you awake again. Can you stop her?' Olivia whispered, not wanting to wake Etta.

No, sweet girl. This is a dream, a true dream, and it's all I can give to you. All I can do is send you the little magic that's left of me. To help you escape.

'But the well-sweetening wore you out.'

As you found with the cat, Olivia, almost always, we have something left, if one we love is threatened, or hurt, or

193

unhappy. Even we don't always know what we can do.

'I suppose I do love Etta... Father, you know about the cat! Have you been watching me, all this time?'

No. I had glimpses in the darkness, here and there. Strange sights. Water, and light and not much else. At first I was angry, and I planned to confine you myself, Olivia, when I was awake again. A princess should not be travelling the canals at night, as you must have been. But the creature with you – his voice sounded so familiar, as though I knew it from another dream. I knew you were safe, and the things he said – they made me think, well, perhaps I was wrong. Perhaps out there was exactly where you should be. Learning about your city, in a way I never have. You must free those children. You were right, the boy can help us.

'But they're in the New Prison, Father. I can't get in there. Even if Lady Sofia hasn't told the guards I'm mad, or whatever lie it is she's planning.'

If it was the creature you were with who calmed the waters, Olivia, then he can do the opposite. Child, I don't have much strength left, and you need my magic more than my advice. Get up, Olivia, and go, now. You'll find that the door is unlocked, and your guard is sleeping.

'But my aunt locked the door, I know she did.'

And this is still my palace, little one. Not hers. Even as I am now, if I say the door is open, then open it shall be.

Across the room, she heard the clicking as the heavy tumblers fell, and she was awake.

'Etta, wake up! We can go. Come on. Oh. Not in this – help me dress, I may need to look like who I am. But nothing too grand, I have to be able to move.'

Etta lay blinking in the tangled bedclothes, half-asleep, and the cat stretched himself luxuriously. Olivia couldn't think of him as Coco now, that was a kitten's name, too sweet for this lithe, strong beast.

'My father unlocked the door for us, Etta. We have to be gone before my aunt comes back. I have a way to break into the prison. I think…'

The palace corridors were quiet, and the few people they met as the hurried to the water doors stared at Olivia in confusion. But no one spoke, until one of Olivia's own ladies-in-waiting ran into them hurrying down the main stairs.

'My lady! Oh!' Lady Anna curtseyed, and rose up staring. 'I'm so glad to see you well!'

'Did my aunt tell you that I was ill?' Olivia said slowly, thinking it out.

'Indeed, my lady. That you had been taken ill after that strange storm on the water yesterday. She had the guards sent out, you know, and a gang of murderous ruffians was rounded up and imprisoned. Lady Sofia told us it was an attempt to assassinate you and the duke!'

'Lady Sofia is wrong,' Olivia snapped. 'About all of it. Do I look ill? Go and tell everyone you meet that I am perfectly well. And that the murderous *ruffians* were just children, playing a silly game with magic they did not understand. I am going to the prison now, to speak with them.'

Lady Anna darted away, and Etta let out the breath she had been holding, in a worried whistle. 'I don't think you should have told her where we're going.'

Olivia sighed. 'Maybe not. But Lady Sofia was always going to find out quite soon, wasn't she? We shall just have to work fast.'

'My lady, how are we getting to the prison?' Etta demanded, as they marched past the guards and stood in the doorway, looking out on to the flooded pavement, and the grey, rain-filled sky over the lagoon. 'You can't just walk in, you know.'

'We're going to break in. From the palace we could go across the Bridge of Sighs, but it would be too well guarded. I would rather do this through a door no one's watching. You have to trust me, Etta. You didn't believe me, about the horse, did you?'

'I've never heard of such a thing... How could there be horses in the water, and no one see them? It makes no sense. It's a fairy tale.'

Olivia smiled as she saw Lucian pacing towards them, knee-deep in the floodwater. It was odd to see him walking with his hooves on the ground, like any other horse. Coco squirmed and spat in Etta's arms, and she winced as he clawed her.

'Coco can see him,' Olivia pointed out to her. 'Etta, I made you a cat out of a cup of chocolate. Yet you still can't believe in a water horse?'

'Have you work for me, my lady?' Lucian leaned

down to rub his muzzle against her hair. 'And who is the cat? They are well known to dislike water.'

'Is he here now?' Etta hissed.

'Yes.' Olivia took her hand, avoiding Coco's claws, and stretched it out to pull Etta's fingers through Lucian's curling mane. 'Can you feel anything?'

'No.'

Olivia frowned. Lucian was so solid, so really there to her. It was hard to understand how almost no one else saw him. She couldn't work out how to make Etta see him too.

Lucian stamped one great foot, the feathers over his hoof dancing and flickering, and the water splashed up, spraying the steps where they stood. 'Did she see that?'

'You got me wet!' Etta snapped, turning so that she was actually looking at Lucian. 'You huge clumsy thing! Oh...'

'You can see him!' Olivia clapped her hands, and then hugged Etta, so tightly that Coco yowled and made a leap to Lucian's back.

'I couldn't quite,' Etta said slowly. 'He was like a

198

shadow. But – oh – now that Coco is standing on him, I can.' She curtseyed. 'My lord…'

'Is she talking to me?' Lucian whispered, ducking his head.

'Yes! Etta, I don't think he's a lord.'

'He ought to be. My lady,' Etta glanced behind them at the guards, gathering by the doors. 'I don't think it will be long before someone summons your aunt.'

Olivia nodded. 'Lucian, we can't ride you, not here. Those soldiers wouldn't understand what was happening. We must take one of these boats tied up here, and row it round into the canal, to the wall of the prison. Jac and Zuzanna are there, and the others, my cousin Zuan tracked them, and they've been shut up inside the prison, all the time we were hunting for them.'

'Stone,' the water horse growled. 'Stone and chains, and dragging them away from the water – that was why I couldn't find them.' He strode out through the canal, heading to the jumble of moored boats, flooded up and away from their mooring posts at the edge of the lagoon.

'Can you break the stones down?' Olivia asked him, as the two girls stumbled through the water,

199

one on each side, clinging to his mane.

Lucian turned back to her, his ears pricked forward in interested surprise. 'Break them?'

'Jac's spell overturned the boats, and broke them up – couldn't your water magic break stone?'

'I'm used to water wearing stone away,' the horse murmured slowly. 'Over the years. But I've never used it to break anything down, deliberately.'

'Won't it work?' Olivia asked him, leaving the mooring rope she'd been pulling at, and looking up at him in dismay.

He didn't answer – instead he bit down on the rope with his yellowish teeth, and pulled the boat away from the post. 'Get in, and hold the oars.'

The two girls and the suspicious cat tumbled clumsily into the boat, and Etta grabbed the oars. Anyone who glanced at the boat might think she was rowing it along, but Lucian still had the rope in his teeth, and he towed them around the front of the flooded pavement into the shadows of the canal that ran between the duke's palace and the prison, dark water glimmering between the high walls.

Olivia looked up at them, stretching tall and smooth and grey on either side, and shook her head. The pale daylight glittering on the lagoon seemed very far away, and the walls of the palace and the prison made an eerie tunnel over their heads. 'It was a stupid idea,' she muttered. 'There's nothing to get hold of.'

But Lucian had let go of the rope, and he stood up in the water with his forefeet pressed against the stones. 'Here. They're here. Hasn't the flood taught you anything? Water can get in anywhere.' His eyes were glittering, and Olivia realised in surprise that he was enjoying himself. He put his head down and snorted, and lashed his mane from side to side, and the water around him began to thrash and boil.

Etta pulled the oars in, and put her hands one each side of the boat, gripping on with whitened fingers. Coco climbed into her lap, and yowled. But Olivia climbed forward into the stern of the tiny, cockleshell craft, and leaned out. She felt the spray rising from the spell on the water, and it dampened her hair and glittered on her cheeks, and she knew that it was strengthening her.

Lucian roared, and pounded on the stones, and they shrieked back at him, grinding and splintering as the water hurled against them, again and again.

The hole came suddenly, with an angry scream of stone, and a rumbling fall as half the wall collapsed into the water.

Lucian reared back, spluttering and sneezing at the dust, and eventually the growling of the stones and the water settled into silence.

'Are they there?' Olivia asked anxiously, and she was answered by a tiny whimpering sound. Then Jac's face, pale and smudged with stone dust, appeared in the opening.

'You!'

'You haven't got time to be angry with her now.' The oldest of the girls, appeared behind him, with Zuzanna in her arms. 'Take her!' she said impatiently, and Lucian nosed the boat forward obediently, and the two girls began to haul the children aboard.

CHAPTER TWELVE

'WHERE ARE YOU TAKING US?' Jac snarled, leaning over from Lucian's neck. The tiny boat could only hold five children at the most, so the water horse looked like some feast day sideshow, with the other five lined up all along his back. They were paddling slowly down the canal, back towards the lagoon, trying to keep to the shadows. But there were other boats passing, and they kept having to stop and hide. They had not made it far away from the prison at all.

Olivia stared back at him open-mouthed, not sure

whether to be angry or embarrassed. She hadn't got much further than knocking down the wall in her plan. Still, surely he could be a little bit grateful for being rescued?

But then, it was clear that he blamed everything on her to start with.

'Since you were foolish enough to show half the city that you can twist the waters to do whatever you want, I'm giving you the chance to redeem yourself,' she told him coldly. 'We're going to send back the floods.'

'What?'

'Or does your water magic only work for hurting people because you're angry?'

'It wasn't like that!'

'It seems that way to me. I didn't deceive you on purpose!'

Lucian looked across at her sharply, and Olivia sighed. 'Well, yes I did. But not to...to play a trick on you, or to cheat you! I was trying to help!' She reached out her hand to him – but it was useless, the boat was too far away. 'I know I don't have any idea what life is like for you. But you don't know about me either. I know you think I'm lucky—'

Jac snorted, and several of the other children narrowed their eyes.

'Yes! Very well, I am lucky. But it isn't all good, you know, being a princess! No one tells me anything! But you did. That's why I came. It wasn't a trick...'

Jac nodded. 'Maybe. But you lied to us.'

'She brought you food. I bet you never thanked her,' Etta put in. 'Oh, don't be silly, my lady, did you think I didn't see you hiding it away? I thought you were playing a game – that it was for the imaginary horse.'

'If we can stop the flooding, everyone will be grateful,' Olivia pleaded. 'Don't you see? Maybe even so grateful you won't have to live under bridges. You're valuable if you can control the water. You'll be paid.'

'With money?' the older girl, they called Marta demanded, looking at her sharply.

'Yes, or things, I don't know. Somewhere to live, maybe. But we have to do it fast – the guards will be coming after you by now and they won't believe us, not even me.'

'But you're a princess,' Marta said. 'Don't they have to do as you tell them?'

'Not if they think I'm ill, and probably half-mad, talking about water horses and beggar magicians. No one will believe us until we show them.'

'She's right,' Jac muttered. 'It's our only chance. They tracked us before and they'll track us again. But I still don't like you,' he added to Olivia. 'I still say you're a liar.'

'Look!' The boat rocked wildly as Zuzanna tried to stand up. 'Look, look, look!'

Swimming towards them was the whole herd of water horses, streaming in from the lagoon in a wave of creamy foam. Lucian neighed proudly, tossing his head as his herd surrounded them, whinnying and nosing at the children, these miraculous children who could see and stroke them.

'Leave the boat,' Lucian told Olivia. 'Ride on us, all of you.'

Zuzanna reached out one tiny, dirty hand and petted the nose of the golden mare Olivia had seen before. The water horse shivered as she felt the child's touch, and her dark eyes shone with joy. She pressed close up against the boat, rocking it a little, and Zuzanna flung her arms around the golden neck, and climbed eagerly on to the horse's back, cooing and giggling at the strangeness of it all. She looked different, up there, Olivia thought, her own eyes bright with unshed tears. The golden mane wrapped round her like a shining garment, and the excitement was flushing her cheeks with colour. She wasn't a pitiful beggar child any longer.

Lucian snorted approvingly as the other children followed Zuzanna's lead. He nudged Etta with his nose. 'Even you must ride, my dear, and the cat.'

'But I can't do water magic,' Etta murmured.

'Perhaps one day you will, when things are set right again, and the magic belongs to all those who can shape it. But even if you have no magic at all, you are the only reason our princess is here. You belong with us now. You and the princess will ride with me.'

'I don't know what to do.' Jac growled it so quietly that Olivia wasn't sure she had heard him. They were pressed up against the palace wall, the children nervous and giggling, and the horses pawing at the water as though they were nervous too. Jac was sitting uncomfortably on the horse next to Lucian, and he looked both worried and angry.

'Neither do I,' Olivia pointed out. 'I've done one spell to keep the waters back, a week or so ago, but it didn't work, did it? It only made the floods go down for a day or so. We probably have to do something different.'

'I thought you knew what we were doing!' Jac hissed.

'I don't either.' Lucian tossed his head. 'But this is stronger than I have felt in years. Don't you feel it too?' He butted Jac playfully with his nose, and the boy yelped, and slid sideways, until Etta caught him.

'You do look stronger,' Olivia said, pretending not to notice Jac's outrage at nearly falling off. 'Your eyes are brighter. And your coat is *glowing*. All of you glow,' she added. 'Surely it can't be long before everyone begins to see you again.' She looked around at them all, realising that the nervous laughter had died away, and the horses were standing still and proud in front of their city. 'We're *all* glowing,' she whispered. 'Look at it, it's like sunlight on the water.'

'There *is* sunlight. The clouds are clearing.' Etta pointed out across the lagoon. 'Look, real sun, it feels like the first time in days.' Strong morning sunlight glittered down across the water, and the pearly light of the horses' coats turned to gold. 'And the moon, my lady, over there above the sandbanks.'

'Send the water out there,' Olivia whispered. 'Back to the sea. The sun and the moon are here with us. The moon controls the tides, and she's here in the daytime. It's a sign. Now! Call on the moon!' She stretched out her hand and seized Jac's, not caring if he hated her. They were together, all of them, wrapped in golden light, ready to send back the water. She could see the children's eyes glittering with excitement, and a little fear, as the power rushed through them.

It was like rolling up a carpet, she thought afterwards. The water seemed to be sucked back, leaving a great expanse of stone in front of them again, steaming in the sunshine. And it went on, and on, until the stones around them began to creak and shift, and Olivia gasped, waking out of that strange golden dream.

'Too much! We sent back too much!' The boats were

209

high and dry in front of her, and the canal that ran between the palace and the prison was hardly a canal at all, just a stream running down a muddy channel. The palace was shaking behind them, and Olivia flung her arms around Lucian's broad neck. She could feel him trembling too – without the water surrounding them, all the horses looked lost.

'An earthquake!' Jac gasped. 'Did we do that?'

Olivia nodded, her eyes wide with horror. 'I suppose we must have done. I didn't mean to! But perhaps all the water was holding everything up. Oh, it's seeping back in already, look. Please hurry, please…'

They watched anxiously, gathering at the edge of the bank and staring down at the water, glittering in the sunlight as it rushed back into its old way. The water horses leapt in after it, kicking joyfully at the ripples.

'It's all coming back again! What if just goes back to being flooded?' one of the boys asked, but Lucian looked up at them, shaking his head, his mane covered in sparkling droplets.

'No, our spell succeeded. It will hold for a while, at least. It was a great work, all of us together.'

Olivia felt Jac squeeze her hand tighter, and she smiled at him, delight and wonder making her forget his anger. He forgot too, for a moment – and then she saw his stubborn distrust come seeping back like the water. He pulled his hand away.

'Will it last?' Olivia asked Lucian quickly, turning away from the ungracious boy.

'I think we have a few days, at least. But we may have to do this again, and we may never be able to stop the flooding for good – the city is half-floating in the sea, after all.'

'Princess Olivia!'

Olivia straightened her spine, and tried to imagine away the stone dust and the water. She turned round regally, and stared at the party of guardsmen in front of her.

'Thank heaven you're safe, my lady!' The captain dropped to one knee before her. 'Your aunt sent us out to look for you. Did you go out for a walk? Did you not see there's been an earthquake, my lady? Half the wall of the New Prison has collapsed! It emptied the Grand Canal!'

'A miracle, my lady,' one of the other soldiers said solemnly. 'It banished the flood waters.'

Olivia stared at them. Had they not seen the magic? The golden glow of the water horses? The power of the spell? Behind her she sensed Jac and the others melting away, ducking behind the beached boats, disappearing, without the reward she had so recklessly promised them.

Nothing had changed. How could that be? Olivia felt her fists clench, the nails digging deeply into her palms. Things could only stay the same if she let them, and now, she knew that she could fight.

CHAPTER THIRTEEN

WALKING BACK INTO THE palace surrounded by the guardsmen did feel very much like they were prisoners. But none of them had dared to lay a hand on her. Olivia smiled sweetly at everyone they passed, trying not to look as though she was in disgrace, but she couldn't appear too light-hearted, not when there had just been an earthquake.

Lady Sofia and the other members of the council were in the Grand Chamber, grouped on the steps in front of her father's throne. Courtiers were talking in anxious huddles all around the room, but they moved apart as Olivia, Etta and their escort came clanking through the hall.

Lady Sofia stood in the centre of the steps, just where Olivia needed to walk to reach her own throne, set beside her father's. She didn't move as Olivia padded through the hall towards her, and Olivia set her teeth together angrily.

As she reached the lowest step to the dais, Olivia swept her best curtsey, dipping her skirts to the perfect height for the sister of the duke. 'My lady…' she murmured, her head bowed. And then she stood up, and bared her teeth in a sweet, war-like smile. 'Would you be so good as to excuse me?' She extended her arm, gesturing to her chair. 'I have been out, inspecting the damage to our city, and speaking with our people. I am somewhat weary.'

Her aunt moved aside, but slowly.

And don't you dare stand in front of me, Olivia snarled silently to herself. *I will make you sorry for all of this, just you wait.* But the snarl was strictly on the inside. Once she was sitting, Olivia stared out at the court, trying to look worried and sympathetic and yet at the same time

– of course – absolutely calm. She suspected that she just looked blank.

'Princess.' Lord Matteo, the councillor who had been so keen to marry her off, swept her a deep bow. 'It has been suggested that we should hold the ritual of the burning boats. To appease the waters.'

Olivia tried not to look surprised. 'Indeed, my lord? But the floods have gone down already.'

'And brought an earthquake after them!' the old man thundered. 'The waters are angry. We must have the burning. You are too young to remember—'

'Lord Matteo!' Olivia snapped. 'I have studied the history of our city. I may not have been alive the last time the rite was performed, but I know of it. I cannot say that it ever seems to have made much difference, according to the accounts I've read.'

'Books!' Lord Matteo shrugged disgustedly. 'I have no time for books.'

Olivia sighed, but under her breath. 'I have no objection to the ceremony, if you think it may help,' she said calmly. 'My Lady Sofia?'

Lady Sofia could do the arguing with Lord Matteo

215

in front of everyone, if she wanted to. And if she didn't have the stomach for fighting with the grizzled old man, then she would have to agree to the burning, and agree with Olivia, in front of all these witnesses.

Her aunt could see quite well what Olivia had done, of course. Her lips thinned so much that they almost disappeared, but she nodded.

'Will you arrange for the ceremony, my lord? For two days' time? Will that be possible?' Olivia gestured gracefully to Lord Matteo, who opened his mouth like a fish, but obviously couldn't see any way to get out of the work of organising the complicated ritual. He muttered something that sounded like yes, bowed, and stomped away.

'I hope you will excuse me now,' Olivia rose. 'I must discuss these new developments with my father.'

Her father? But I thought the duke was unconscious again?

Yes, that's what Lady Sofia said.

Good gracious, the child is filthy! Look at the state of her!

And where did she get that strange brown cat?

Did you know, Lady Bel was telling me…

And more, and more, and more, the whispers battering against her as she walked to the doors. *Sometimes*, Olivia thought as Etta slammed the doors behind her, *I envy Jac and Marta and Zuzanna and all of them. Could living under a bridge really be any worse than that?*

The red-gold flames flickered, then died, and the blackened timbers shuddered, disappearing under the dark water of the lagoon. Olivia tried not to shiver as a cold wind cut through her thin, lace-trimmed gown. Even though she couldn't see that burning the boats would make the slightest bit of difference, she didn't want anyone to think she had jinxed the ritual by not paying proper attention.

She had not seen Jac and the others since the morning of their rescue – and the earthquake – two days before. And she had only seen Lucian in passing glimpses, never to ride with. She hadn't dared to leave the palace and give Lady Sofia any chance of twisting her night-time journeys into something suspicious, or even treasonous.

The spell had gone from her window, and neither her aunt nor her cousin had said anything about that night. It was as if the encounter in her room had never happened.

They were waiting. Olivia knew that they would strike again – of course they would. They were storing it up, hoarding all their information for the right time. And for now, Lady Sofia just pretended to be as sweet as she always had. Olivia wondered how she had ever been deceived.

She wandered through her lessons and her visits to her father in a sort of anxious dream. She wanted to shout at all her tutors, insist that they stop the dreary recitations of wars and trades and marriages, and to demand that instead they search the oldest, most crumbling papers in the library for the stories of the water horses. It still made her angry – and desperately sad – that they had been forgotten. She was determined that they would be brought back to their proper place. But when she tried to ask her tutors about them, she could see from their smiles and sideways looks that they thought she was being childish.

It would happen, she told herself, leaning out of her bedroom window on the morning after they had burned the boats, and laughing sadly as she watched Lucian frisking in the water beneath her, kicking up the spray to dampen her hair. She would make it happen. Her father already knew that she had met some sort of water creature. He said he had heard Lucian's voice. It had reminded him of a dream, he thought, but Olivia wondered if it was something he had always known, deep down; part of their family history, buried deep inside them all. When he woke up – *when* – then they would tell everyone. She would make them see.

But until then she was lost, a princess, but with the very timbers of her palace still rocking and sliding beneath her. Since the earthquake, the rumours of the duke's approaching death seemed to be accepted as fact, despite Olivia's daily promises in the Grand Chamber and at the meetings of the Council of Ten that his health was improving. She wasn't really a very good liar.

'I have to go to the audience chamber, and show myself to the court,' she explained to Lucian. 'Everyone is convinced that my father is dying.' She tried not to let her voice shake, but it was hard. She had hardly felt her father's magic since the night her aunt and Zuan had attacked her and Etta, and she couldn't help thinking that he had given her the last of his strength. And what had she done with it? With her father still alive, Olivia's strength in the court was only what she could persuade the Council of Ten to give her – which was practically nothing, since the council were all under the thumb of Lady Sofia, and even if they hadn't been, they still thought of Olivia as a little girl, not even old enough to be married, let alone rule a city. The court felt like a squirming nest of worms that she was supposed to carry with her – seething and muttering, and coiling away into dark corners to plot. She was losing them, and she knew it. It was more important than ever for her to be there, to be smiling, to look like a princess. She had to try to keep the court on her side, until her father awoke again, and she could explain the magic of the water horses properly to him. Olivia was sure that if she and her father worked together with Lucian and the others, and with the children from the bridge, they could build some sort of protection from the floods. There might be others in the city who had the magic buried deep inside them, those who loved the water. Even if they couldn't hold the flooding back completely, they'd be able to find a way to guide the water where it would do least damage. But she would never be able to convince the Council of Ten without her father's help. Until he woke up, she had to keep smiling and lying.

All she wanted to do was to be out in the city, her real city, on the water.

She stepped back a little from the window, dragging herself away reluctantly from the shining canal, and the glow of pale light that was the horse. 'Lady Sofia sent a message saying that one of the foreign ambassadors has asked her for a meeting, that he's demanded we give way on the trade controls he's negotiating. They're all waiting to pounce, like vultures. I have to be there, Lucian, I can't let anyone say that I'm weak or ill as well. I have to go now.'

'Can't you come riding with me instead?' the water horse begged. 'Do these trade treaties and ambassadors really matter more than the magic and the deep waters? With both our magic together, we could hide you.

221

You've never come down the canals with me in daylight, not just for fun. The sun's out – the water's glittering...'

Olivia sighed, and shook her head. 'I know it is. It's glittering beautifully all across the piazza. The waters are rising again, and I have to go and pretend that everything is fine, and that we will solve it all. *Just wait another day, or two or three, or perhaps a week, and everything will be just as you remember it.* Which will never happen, because the entire court seems to have forgotten that the city has ever flooded before. I feel like I say the same things every day,' she murmured. 'One day soon, I'll ride with you, Lucian. I promise. Goodbye!' But soon felt very far away.

As she took her place in the Grand Chamber, breathing rather fast due to the tight lacing of her corseted dress, Olivia felt there was something different about the room, and the people in it. There was an expectation, something almost hungry.

She lifted her chin a little higher, feeling the weight of the heavy pearls Etta had woven into her hair. Although they had never discussed it, both of them knew that she had to make up for her damp dress and wild hair on the day of the earthquake. She must be exquisite, whenever she was seen. She had stopped telling Etta to let out her laces.

She glanced around the room, trying to see where that strange excitement was coming from. Even Etta could feel it, she realised. Her maid was standing closer than usual, almost at her shoulder instead of behind the throne. And she had her hand up to her face.

The bruise had faded now, so that it was just the faintest yellow tinge, but Olivia was sure it still ached, even though Etta never complained. And Coco was hissing, a low persistent hiss. Olivia could see his tail twitching rhythmically from side to side.

Zuan. Of course. He was standing quite close, at the bottom of the dais, and that dark, delighted sense was coming off him in waves. Something was wrong. He was going to make something wrong.

Olivia patted her little mask pendant, and sent the magic swirling round all three of them. She would not let him attack Etta or Coco again. She murmured the same soft words about her father's recovery, and the rising floods – and they sounded useless, even to her.

223

She told herself that she was not frightened, but it was a lie. She was waiting for Zuan to strike.

One of the lords from the council was rambling through a long complaint about the flood damage to his palazzo, which just made Olivia think of little Zuzanna, who'd never known a home with walls.

'My lord.'

The elderly councilman broke off, surprised, and turned short-sightedly to see who had interrupted him.

'Here, my lord.' Zuan bowed deep. 'I sympathise with your loss. But I am angry, sir, angry as well. I suspect that these floods are not natural. I think they have been sent against us. I have been speaking to those of you who were injured in the attack during the sweetening of the wells. As I was myself. You know, of course, that the criminals responsible escaped from the New Prison during the earthquake.'

Olivia tucked her hands into the silken folds of her skirt. They were so cold. Zuan had been waiting for the opportunity to say all this. He had learned it off by heart, she decided. There was something practised about the way he was gesturing, and turning to those about him, catching their eyes, taking them along with him. This was a polished performance, and he had been well coached.

'Rogue magic, we said, my lords and ladies. Unexplained. Never to be repeated, the ruffians long gone.'

Ruffians! Serious, worried Marta? Zuzanna, that baby?

'But it can be explained, and they have not gone. They're still here, waiting for another chance. Sending the floods to work against the city. Waiting for my lady, the princess, to betray us. It may even be that the earthquake was not natural – that it was a cruel weapon used against our city, and our people.'

Olivia stared coldly at him. She had to ask. There was no way not to. But it was like stepping into a spider's web, sticky and dangerous, with the spider waiting for her to tangle herself up.

'What is this strange accusation, Lord Zuan?'

'Alas, my lady, I fear you have been deceived, by a rogue. The boy who worked the spell that day, and upset the boats. He was trying to drown us! Many of us who were there that day saw how you reacted to the water magic. You knew him.' He looked round sadly at the avidly listening crowd behind him. 'With her father so ill, you see, she has not been as closely watched as she should have been. My dear mother herself caught the princess *climbing back in through her bedroom window.'*

What was so awful was that he hadn't said anything that wasn't true. He was even right about the earthquake. But somehow he was weaving the truth into something sickening and bad. Lady Sofia was crying – delicately.

'As you know, it has long been the duke's wish that in time, Princess Olivia and I should be married.' Zuan's voice quickened with a horrid eagerness, and Olivia felt Etta seize her hand. 'I fear that something like this will only happen again. I beg you, my lady.' He bowed to Olivia, and as he stood up, she caught the terrifying glitter of his yellowish eyes. 'Let us be married at once, so that my mother and I can guide you away from whatever evil has possessed you.'

Olivia laughed. It was so difficult that it almost hurt, but she made it sound real. Real enough. 'Lord Zuan!

You honour me. I am possessed, and in league with a gang of rogues, but you *still* wish to marry me?'

A little ripple of giggling ran round the chamber – mostly from the women, Olivia thought. Girls who had seen Zuan for the cruel bully that he was.

'I am afraid I cannot return the favour, my lord,' she went on, taking courage from that sweet laughter. 'I am obedient to my father's wishes, as always, and I have spoken with him about my marriage. He and I are quite agreed. I will never, ever marry you.'

CHAPTER FOURTEEN

PERHAPS IT HAD BEEN A MISTAKE. Perhaps she should never have said it so openly. But she couldn't stand the way that all the older members of the court had seemed to be nodding and approving. And that they seemed to think she would be lucky to have him! As though it was settled. No one had ever asked her! They didn't know what Zuan was like.

But now they were all staring at her, the air fizzing with intrigue – and disapproval. How dared she? When she had just been accused of such shameful behaviour too! Perhaps she was in league with those

228

magicians? It was probably all a plot against her father!

'My lady.' It was Lord Matteo – but he was not speaking to Olivia. 'My Lady Sofia. When did you last see your brother, His Grace the duke?'

'Yesterday, my lord.'

'Is he recovering, as Princess Olivia tells us?'

Lady Sofia stared back at him, and then glanced solemnly all around the room. Olivia could feel the triumph rolling off her in sweet, sickening waves. At last, the power she had envied her brother all these years was to be hers. She was so close. What was she about to do? Olivia swallowed, her mouth suddenly dry – it had come, the moment she had been dreading – and she wasn't ready. Her allies were street children, and a fairy tale, and none of them were here, just her and Etta. She was no match for the grandly dressed courtiers, angry and frightened as they were.

'No, my lord,' Lady Sofia murmured sadly. 'I am beginning to fear that he will never wake up.'

'So the princess has been lying to us?'

'Why is my aunt's opinion more to be believed than mine, Lord Matteo?' Olivia asked, her voice a quiet hiss that was the only way she could stop it from trembling.

'Because you have lied, and because you are a child,' he snapped, in a tone he would never have dared to use before. 'A motherless child whose magic has not been properly controlled. You have run wild, and this is the result. We may never get to the truth of your doings. I hope and pray that you have not used your unnatural spells against your father, and brought shame to our city.'

He bowed low to Lady Sofia – lower than he should have done, Olivia thought, that deep, fearful emptiness opening inside her again. He was behaving as if her aunt was duchess regent already. Was he part of the plan all along?

'We are lucky,' he proclaimed, mounting the steps of the dais, 'that despite the duke's illness, and his daughter's treachery, we still have those of the royal blood who are fit to rule. Lord Zuan was brave enough to speak against his cousin's wickedness, and his mother will guide him until he is old enough to rule alone. I say we depose the duke, and this shamed girl should no longer be his heir.'

'How dare you suggest such a thing?' Olivia cried furiously, leaping up. 'The treachery is yours, not mine at all. You cannot just declare that my father is no longer the duke!'

'The council can, my lady,' another of the ten reminded her, with a bow. 'If we are all agreed, and we can prove it necessary. We met this morning.'

'They can't do this,' Etta whispered, under the uproar in the hall, as the gathered crowd surged around, arguing with each other and the council members. 'Use your magic, my lady. Fight back!'

'I can't,' Olivia muttered, glancing wildly from side to side. There was a horrible eagerness in the chamber now, the shouting was quieting to a low mutter, as everyone waited to see what would happen. 'Not without hurting the other people in the room. That's why they did it here, even though it was a risk… They knew I wouldn't. I can't believe that they would do this. I could have sworn that Lord Matteo was loyal to my father, even if I didn't like him.'

'Perhaps he's been too close to Lady Sofia,' Etta said, shuddering.

Olivia turned to stare at her. 'You think she bewitched them all?'

'Why not? She did it to you for long enough! And like you said, he was always loyal before. My lady, can we get out?'

Olivia looked around at the doors, each with their guards. They were dressed only in ceremonial uniforms, more gold and tassels than useful armour, but they had pikes, and swords at their hips. 'No.' She swallowed, because her throat felt dry. 'You had better go now, Etta. Slip out quietly. Take your mother from the laundry and go. Get out of the city, if you can. They'll want to make sure you can't talk. I'm not letting them shut you up in the New Prison too.'

'Don't be stupid! My lady.' Etta glanced at her sideways, and swallowed. Even when they were about to be thrown in jail as traitors, she found it hard not to be polite.

'What are they going to do?' Olivia whispered, pressing closer to Etta, and slipping her hand into her maid's. Holding Etta's hand stopped her own shaking quite so much. 'I don't think they can hurt me – or, or worse. I don't think the court would let them. Or the people – I don't think they could hate me that much, could they? But if they imprison me, they'll never be safe. They know I'll work out some way to escape by magic.'

'They've got to get rid of you somehow,' Etta agreed.

'I think marrying Zuan was my last chance.' Olivia gave a sharp, angry gasp of laughter. 'Well, I did think it was a fate worse than death... I do hope I was right.'

'She's conspiring with her maid!' Zuan shrieked suddenly, making Olivia look up at him in shock. 'Look at them, she's another accomplice. Stand back, my lords and ladies, watch for her! Watch for that unnatural creature by her side!'

'He's only a cat,' Etta muttered. 'But then, that beast knows he's already killed him once. I suppose that does make him a little unnatural.'

The courtiers were scurrying back against the walls, as though they expected Olivia to throw thunderbolts, and strike them down. When Coco padded forward, at least one elderly lady fainted. Olivia and Etta were abandoned on the dais, with only Zuan standing in front of them.

'Murdering liar,' Olivia said to him conversationally.

'I haven't murdered anyone.'

'Yet.'

'This cannot go on!' Lady Sofia cried, and Olivia winced. Her aunt's voice shook and broke dramatically, and she was leaning against Lord Matteo as though she was half-fainting. She was so believable – she didn't need the magic to make people do what she wanted. 'We cannot let a child frighten us like this – and know that she will only be stronger as she grows older.'

An anxious storm of whispering broke out at that, and Olivia glanced at the doors again. What were they going to do to her? She couldn't believe that Lady Sofia was planning to attack her here, in front of everyone. Weren't there any spells she could use to stop this? A binding spell to shut her up, even? But if she did that, Lady Sofia's supporters would only say that it proved their story true – Olivia *was* dangerous. She was attacking her family.

She was caught.

'The princess has brought this flooding on the city. Lord Matteo was right – her magic is not natural, and she is too strong. She has stolen the powers from her father, and drained him almost to death. We cannot let her steal away the magic from our city. She must give it back!' Lady Sofia raised her arms to the ceiling, shrieking the words, and several of the courtiers close to her began to stamp, and cheer.

'Spells. I can see her doing it. She's whipping them all up...' Olivia muttered. 'Oh, why didn't I bewitch some people too?'

'You have the horses,' Etta reminded her, but she didn't sound very confident about it.

'And a gang of street children, who hate me anyway.' Olivia shook her head. 'She's winning...'

'Such cruel treatment of her father can only be balanced by the greatest sacrifice.' Lady Sofia lowered her voice almost to a whisper, so that everyone in the Grand Chamber was quiet, desperate to hear what she was about to say. 'The burning of the boats failed because the princess was working against us. But there is another ritual. Darker magic – a spell that I have always condemned! But now I see why it was necessary, so many hundreds of years ago. A terrible sacrifice.'

Olivia went white, her knees buckling beneath her. She staggered a little, clutching Etta's arm. She knew what her aunt meant. She had read about it, long ago, and even when she was her father's favoured little daughter it had given her nightmares. She had asked him about the story, even shown him the book, and he had laughed. It would never happen again, he'd told her. (He wasn't even sure it had happened the last time, the book was so old, and full of fanciful reports.) Besides, it could only have happened (if indeed it had) because there was a spare princess, with three older brothers, and a baby sister too, for useful marriage marketing. It would never happen when there was only one... And that had made him sad, thinking about her mother, so Olivia had gone away, and tried to forget about it. She had tried not to imagine the water, closing over her face... She had almost managed, until now.

'It isn't a terrible sacrifice to you at all,' Olivia pointed out in a shaking voice. 'It's exactly what you want to do. It's almost as if you planned it, really.' It wasn't helping her to be rude to her aunt, but if they were going to drown her anyway, she wasn't going to let them do it without complaining. And she wasn't going to cry and scream and plead, either. 'Etta, please try to get away,' she whispered.

'Seize the traitor, before she escapes!' Zuan screamed, leaping up the steps and grabbing Olivia's arm. She smacked him in the face, not with any magic at all, and he stared at her in shock – he almost let her go. For all his strength, he never fought with people who were allowed to fight back. But Zuan was followed by several others, Lord Matteo among them, and Olivia found herself held fast. Her magic was leaping inside her, she could feel it pressing against her skin, and she was so tempted to fling herself away from them in a blur of angry light. But it would burn them, and break them, and she couldn't bring herself to make her aunt's words true.

'Signor Francisco, bind her.'

It was clever of Lady Sofia to pretend that she needed the doctor to do it, Olivia thought dazedly, as the old man passed his hands in front of her face, and she felt the magic begin to seal itself down inside her, locking her away in a prison of her own body. Of course it would have been easy for her aunt, now that Olivia was so tightly held, and could be forced to look into her eyes. But to use a doctor seemed gentler, and fairer.

He hated to do it, she could tell. He knew her a little, from all her visits to her father. He did not think she had been stealing the duke's magic, Olivia was sure. He would have seen the traces of her power if she had, when he used his own healing spells upon the duke. But he was old, and tired, and one man's voice would never stand alone against all these others. She could see it all in his eyes, his sadness, his guilt, and something else, something she didn't recognise. Probably fear. Who was it he was frightened of? Her or Lady Sofia? It was important…

And then the blackness swept down over her, and all the colour and brightness of her magic disappeared.

Even though she was unconscious, the words still reached her.

Poor child – so young!

She doesn't look like a traitor. She never said anything

238

treacherous when we waited upon her. We just gossiped, and listened to the lute-player, and sewed. She sews ever so nicely…

Don't be silly, Julia, what does a traitor look like? And I hope she didn't speak of treachery to you! Wicked little creature, sitting sewing while she was planning to steal her father's magic!

I didn't, Olivia tried to say. *You have it all wrong. And you'll regret it, before long, when you see what she's like… Wait and see…Oh, Etta! I hope you got away!*

The coolness of the breeze half-woke her, and the spray upon her face. For a moment, she thought she must be riding with Lucian and the others, through the city in the sunshine, just as she had promised.

Her eyes flickered, and half-opened, but she couldn't move her fingers, or even open her mouth. She was still imprisoned by the doctor's spell. *It's like the drug they give you before they pull your teeth*, she thought dreamily. *Something to stop you screaming, as they throw you in the water…They have musicians too, so as to cover up the noise…*

She was lying on some sort of table, and the sunlight was sparkling on the golden trappings all around her. The barge. Back where it had all started, that first day, when Etta had shown her the listening spells…

Where *was* Etta? A little of the dreamy feeling floated away, and Olivia's thoughts grew clearer. The anger came back, stirring the magic inside her, and urging her to fight against the binding spell. Her aunt was trying to steal the city – and she was winning! In a few minutes, Olivia would be gone, and Venice would belong to them, to Lady Sofia and Zuan, who had beaten Etta, and tried to kill Coco. How could she leave *them* to rule her city?

Olivia tried to struggle, to sit upright. How angry she would be, if they had hurt Etta again!

I'm stronger than that old doctor, she thought to herself. *Lady Sofia will be sorry that she didn't deal with me herself. There's water all around this ship, and the water belongs to me!*

The faint, ethereal music was rising, the voices twirling round each other in counterpoint. The ritual was coming to its height, and Olivia still couldn't move.

She would be awake enough to know that she was drowning, but not to save herself.

'Tie the stones around her ankles.'

Olivia shuddered as she heard Zuan's voice. He was trying so hard to sound serious, but he couldn't hold back the note of glee. He must have dreamed of getting rid of her like this for years. She wondered if he was to be the one who threw her in the water.

They were lifting her now. She could see a glimpse of her own arm, now that her head was falling back. She had always hated this purple dress. It made her skin look yellowish. She still couldn't move, however hard she wrenched at the bindings inside her. *This is what it must have been like for Father, all this time*, she thought, and tears welled out of her eyes.

'She's awake,' someone whispered fearfully. 'Look at her eyes.'

'Poor pretty little thing…' An older, gruff voice; a guard, half-familiar. He had stood watch outside her father's rooms. 'She's crying… This ain't right. I don't believe she was stealing magic from her father. I seen her with him. She was his little dear. I'll have no part in this, my lord. You find someone else to carry her.'

'And you'll be dismissed!' Zuan, high and angry.

'Better that than a murderer. That's what this is. And more than half the city will think the same.'

Is that true? Olivia wondered, as the sea-breeze ruffled her hair. *Or will they think it's worth it, to keep the water out of their houses?*

The fall came quickly – perhaps Zuan thought the others were listening to the old guardsman, and he didn't want to risk any more mutineers. It wasn't like her fall from the window – then she'd struggled, flailing her arms and fighting against the air. This time she crumpled and fell like a stone, staring up at the blue sky above her. She hardly felt the cold of the water – just the pleasant shiver as it slid silkily over her, and sealed her away again.

Lucian said that I had water magic, she thought, sinking as though in a dream. Jade-green water idled past her, patterned with bubbles. *He said that I was strong, and he said I belonged to the water, and the water belonged to me. If I fight, I can break the spell.*

But I'm not sure if I want to.

It's so hard. Everything's hard. Father is dying – however much I've sworn he isn't. Perhaps Lady Sofia would be better at ruling the city after all.

She coughed, and breathed sea water, and coughed again. *Zuan, though. He'd be duke after her. What will he do to Etta, and Jac? And what if they catch the children, and little Zuzanna tells them all the secrets? What if she tells them about the pretty water horses?*

I promised Lucian I'd ride with him in the sun.

I promised!

Last time she'd been drowning, Lucian had saved her. This time, she would save herself, and then she would go back and save everybody else. She had promised. All at once she remembered the sunlight glittering on the water when she had last seen him, only that morning, a few hours before. It seemed like years. She saw the diamond sparkles Lucian's hooves flung up as he pawed the surface, snorting and flinging back his head. That was hers. No one could take that away from her. The binding was useless – Signor Francisco had not even wanted to do it, she realised now. She tore it away, laughing inside, and the magic came surging back up inside her, filling her all through. It felt stronger than ever before – and she was awake.

The icy coldness of the sea hit her all at once, and she fought it, struggling back up towards the glittering sunlight, and clawing against the water, until she broke the surface, her fingers tangled in white hair.

'Were you there all the time?' she gasped, staring into Lucian's dark eyes.

'I could have lifted you out of the water, but I couldn't break the spell. You had to do that for yourself. And you did.' He nudged her lovingly, his great muzzle stroking her cheek like velvet. 'My princess. I knew you would have the magic – you just needed to call up your full strength.'

'So you were going to let me drown if I didn't set myself free?' Olivia demanded indignantly.

'Certainly not.' Lucian snorted. 'I was just going to let you drown a bit more. Now climb on to my back, my lady, and smile.'

Olivia flung her arm around his neck, and rested her face against the warm white hair. 'No, hadn't you better hide me somehow, and take me back to the palace?

244

I need to see my father one more time – then I'll have to find somewhere to go. Perhaps I can find Jac, and ask him. They might even let me stay with them. Except it wouldn't be fair, if I'm fighting against my aunt. They would be caught up in it too. It would be better if everyone thought I was really dead, then I can work against Lady Sofia better, probably.'

'He told us you'd come back, but I couldn't believe him. Oh, my lady, when I saw you fall...' Etta's voice was shaking, and so were her hands when she clutched at Olivia's arm. Olivia's maid was perched high on the neck of a slim white water horse, with Coco in front of her clinging for dear life to its mane. His whiskers were slicked back with spray, and he was looking at Olivia as though this was all her fault, and he would like to bite her. 'We thought you were gone.' Then Etta shook her head, almost crossly, and tried to drag Olivia out of the water. 'Hurry up, my lady! People are pointing at us. Get up on his back and wave, can't you?'

'Etta, where did you come from?' Olivia smiled at her wearily. She was so confused. Etta was scowling now, but Olivia could tell that she was speaking so sharply because she had been desperately frightened. She had thought she was watching Olivia die.

'Everyone needs to see that it was you that brought the horses, my lady, hurry!' Etta hauled at her, pushing her on to Lucian's back in a most undignified way.

'They can see you?' Olivia whispered, looking at the lines of faces along the side of the barge, and the hundreds of little boats her aunt had summoned for the ritual. No one was talking. Not a word. They watched in silence as the horses ranged themselves in front of the barge.

'They did it.' Etta pointed behind her to the other horses, each with a ragged child on its back. 'Made up a spell, *he* said.'

'You could have done it, if you'd tried,' Jac told her, smirking a little. 'It's in all of us, I reckon.'

'You've decided you are a magician, then,' Olivia said slowly.

'Maybe a bit.' He shrugged. 'When I feel like it. And since you'd been stupid enough to get yourself caught, we thought we better do something.'

'Go along by the side of the barge,' Etta said firmly.

'Closer in. My lady, watch out for your cousin. And your aunt. I'd never have got away from that boy if Coco hadn't clawed the side of his face to ribbons.' She smiled grimly. 'We paid him back.'

'You got away. And then you went to find Lucian,' Olivia murmured.

'He found *me*.'

'I'm afraid your palace is a little bit more flooded than it was.' The great horse craned around to nuzzle her cheek. 'I had to get inside so I could find you. But that spell made you hard to track. It hid your magic from me. Etta told me they had summoned the barge.'

'You all came…' Olivia murmured, as the herd of white and golden horses trotted proudly through the flickering waves around the barge. She heard gasps, and whispers of delight, and hands reached down. Jac and his horse sprang out of the water, spray trailing after them, rainbow-shining in the sun.

'Lady Sofia!' Lucian cried. 'I call the Lady Sofia!'

Olivia wrapped her hands tighter in his mane, her heart thumping. She watched her aunt move slowly down the side of the barge until she stood in front of them. Lady Sofia's face was white, and her eyes had lost their golden softness, dulling to a brown like dry pebbles.

'You have no power in my city,' the horse called up. 'Duke Angelo is weak, but still alive. He is awake, in the palace, and his magic is growing strong again. I can feel it – his magic is true, and his daughter will be even stronger than he is.'

'He's awake?' Olivia whispered, clutching even more tightly at Lucian's mane. 'Are you sure? He's well?'

'Awake, and watching you. He has some sort of scrying spell, he's gazing into the floodwater,' Lucian murmured. 'Sit straight, dear one. Your father can see you now.' He reared up, striking clouds of spray with his forefeet, and roared at Lady Sofia again. '*He* is the duke, not your brat. You tried to steal a throne for your son, and the pair of you tried to murder my princess.'

'Not murder…' Lady Sofia said weakly, licking her dry lips. Lucian seemed to terrify her.

'Murder. And disguised by cowards to look like justice. We have lived among you in the waters of this city for hundreds of years. It was our land, before it was ever yours. And we say: go.'

'Go!' shrieked Jac's horse, and the others joined in, whinnying and snorting, so that Lady Sofia fell back from the rail in terror.

'*This* is your princess!' Lucian roared. 'Arrest that woman and her son, and take them out of my city. I will not have them here!' He reared up again, his hooves smashing the water into great waves, tall enough to rock the barge as the oarsmen set it backing away. Olivia could see the soldiers closing in to seize her aunt and Zuan. Lord Matteo was watching, with the strangest expression of bewilderment. As though he was waking from a spell too.

'Exile!' Olivia heard him say it clearly, the words drifting on the wind. 'Confine Lady Sofia and her son to their rooms. Guard them well. We will consult with the princess over what to do next. The white horse is right – those creatures cannot stay here.'

Lucian snorted approvingly, pawing at the water, and shaking his mane. Then the water horse turned to look at Olivia again, the angry glitter gone from his eyes. He glanced at her sideways, almost shyly, and swished his tail through the water, casting up a sparkling foam. 'The sun's still shining,' he murmured, as she threw her arms around his neck, and buried her face in the damp sweetness of his mane.

THE END

Don't miss more MAGIC in the
stunning sequel…

The
Mermaid's
Sister

Coming soon

Read on for a sneak peek…

MIA WATCHED AS THEY WALKED away from her, the golden embroidery on her mother's dress glinting in the low morning sunlight. She didn't understand where they were going, or why her mother had stroked her cheek, and wound her fingers so tightly in Mia's hair. Mia had traced her fingers over the embroidery again, and rubbed her face against its beautiful roughness.

They were too far away, making for a boat pulled up at the jetty, a dark-cloaked soldier standing by to hand them in. Mama was leaning on Zuan, as though she was too tired to walk, and his head was hanging. A sudden panic seemed to rise up inside Mia, and she took one stumbling step forward, before she was caught, and held. The glittering threads of the embroidery pulled at her, tugging at something deep inside. Then they stretched, thinner and thinner – almost too slight and delicate to see, but still there, wrapped round her heart.

'Stay here with me, Mia,' her cousin murmured, wrapping Mia in her arms. 'You can't go with them, I'm so sorry.'

'Mama,' she whispered. But her mama didn't look back, and the boat crept away across the shining water of the lagoon, swallowed up into the white sunlight.

It took a long time to understand why they had gone. Years of whispers, and sideways looks, and turning away. It was a statue that explained it, in the end. Her cousin, on a stone plinth in the piazza, looking out over the water, where Mia's mother and brother had disappeared. Her face was hard and gleaming in bronze, and her enamelled eyes glittered. There were other statues of Olivia, and portraits too, with softer, sweeter gazes. But to Mia, that hard bronze face was the one that seemed the most like her. Especially once she knew what her cousin had done.

The inscription read, *Her Most Serene Highness, Princess Olivia, with gratitude, on the occasion of the banishment of the usurper.*

Mia had walked past it for years, only smiling at her cousin's fussy hairstyle, and the way there always seemed to be a huge seagull sitting on her shoulder. The statue was spelled not to let them land, but the seagulls didn't care. They ate everything, and Mia suspected they had simply eaten the spell.

She first understood when she was only a few years younger than Olivia had been when the statue was made. 'What's an usurper?' she asked her lady-in-waiting, as they passed the statue. 'And what did Cousin Olivia do?'

The lady-in-waiting was a dim, pretty girl from a good family, and she didn't know what to say. She stuttered something, and tried to hurry Mia away, but Mia stood her ground, even more determined now.

'Well? What does it mean?' She looked the statue up and down, and her cousin's stubborn, serious face glared back at her.

'A usurper is someone who tries to steal the throne,

Lady Mia,' the lady-in-waiting whispered at last.

'And Olivia stopped them?'

'Yes, my lady.'

'Oh…' Why would that make the girl blush and stammer so? Mia frowned, and then the whispering and indrawn breaths she had heard for so long seemed to shift and settle again inside her head.

Poor child…

I'm amazed the duchess was gracious enough to let her stay. For all they say she was too young to know, she was bewitched by her mother, wasn't she?

Who knows when she might decide to betray her cousin?

Bad blood, it always comes out.

Discover the rest of Mia's incredible story in

The Mermaid's Sister

Holly Webb is an internationally bestselling author, whose books have sold over two million copies worldwide. Her much-loved *Animal Stories* a publishing phenomenon and to date she has penned over one hundred books for children.

The Water Horse is the first in a new series that combines the things that Holly loves most: magic, historical drama and animals.

www.holly-webb.co.uk